DO NOT REMOVE
CARDS FROM POCKET

Toshio Mori in his study, working on a story. Mid-forties.

Yokohama, California

by
Toshio Mori

Introduction to the Original Edition, by William Saroyan

Introduction to the 1985 Edition, by Lawson Fusao Inada

University of Washington Press

Seattle and London

Acknowledgment is made to the following publications for their permission to reprint some of the stories in this book: *The Coast, Common Ground, Current Life, Pacific Citizen, New Directions, The Clipper, The Writer's Forum, Trek,* and *Matrix.*

Copyright © 1949 by the Caxton Printers, Ltd.
"Standing on Seventh Street: An Introduction to the 1985 Edition," by Lawson Inada, copyright © 1985 by the University of Washington Press
Originally published by the Caxton Printers, Ltd., Caxton, Idaho. University of Washington Press paperback edition published by arrangement with Caxton, 1985
Second printing, 1993
Printed in the United States of America

Library of Congress Cataloging-in-Publication Data
Mori, Toshio, 1910–1980
  Yokohama, California.
  Reprint. Originally published: Caldwell, Idaho: Caxton Printers, 1949.
  Includes William Saroyan's introduction to the original edition.
  I. Title
PS3563.087163Y6   1985   813'.54   84–21987
ISBN 0–295–96167–8 (pbk.)

The paper used in this publication meets the minimum requirements of American National Standard for Information Sciences—Permanence of Paper for Printed Library Materials, ANSI Z39.48–1984. ∞

Standing on Seventh Street

I. The Book

This is the book—the first real Japanese-American book. This is the book—the one people ignored and rejected. This is the book—the one that "was postponed." This is the book—by "the first real Japanese-American writer." This is the book—a monument, a classic of literature.

This is more than a book. This is legacy, tradition. This is the enduring strength, the embodiment of a people. This is the spirit, the soul. This is the community, the identity. This is the pride, the joy, the love.

This is *Yokohama, California.* This *is* Japanese America.

II. Moving Literature

Yokohama, California is a moving book, a heartfelt book of enjoyment and emotion. There is power in the pages; there is courage, conviction. There is also a tremendous sense of humor—the joy of the human condition. It is the most human of qualities to laugh, to be able to laugh, to recognize the wisdom of humor, the humor of wisdom.

It might be said that this book is in the time-honored *shibai* tradition of folk drama and humorous skits. Not all the stories are meant to be funny, but in many of them the humorous characters and situations are the very source of wisdom and depth. Stories like "The Trees" or "The Eggs of the World" are funny because, unfortunately, the people don't seem to be capable of understanding each other. They talk but they don't listen; they can't communicate. Readers will laugh with recognition; these are learning situations; they happen all the time.

Toshio Mori is an exemplary teacher, and a writer of great compassion. There is not a mean bone in all of *Yokohama, California*. His is the gentle humor of respect, not the cynical laughter of ridicule. As Nisei writer Hisaye Yamamoto noted in her Introduction to Mori's other collection of stories, *The Chauvinist,* there is a "Zen flavor" to the man's work. This makes good sense, and it shows; it might be said that Toshio Mori came from "laughing stock." The humor is there, but it runs deep.

One of the funniest and most moving stories is "The Seventh Street Philosopher," featuring Motoji Tsunoda, an old bachelor, a laundryman who considers himself a philosopher in "the tradition and the

*Asian American Studies Center, University of California, Los Angeles, 1979.

blood flow of Shakyamuni, St. Shinran, Akegarasu, and Motoji Tsunoda. He is not joking when he says this." He takes himself seriously, too seriously, perhaps, and is always ready to lecture to anyone who will or won't listen. His favorite topic?—"What is there for the individual to do today." He becomes a pathetic, ridiculous figure when only eleven people ("counting the two babies") show up in a rented auditorium to hear him speak; he is laughable; he drones on and on as the people yawn and snore. Motoji Tsunoda is ridiculous—like the idea of one hand clapping in a forest. However, as depicted by Mori, there is more to the man than appearances; there was "something worth while for everyone to hear and see, not just for the eleven persons in the auditorium but for the people of the earth." And the "laugh" is actually on everyone else; the "joke" is on those who "missed the boat," who did not have the sense, or grace, to attend. Motoji Tsunoda was a man of "courage and bravery."

There is a very expensive lesson to be learned here. It might have been funny to some that Toshio Mori, the nurseryman down the street, spent all of his spare time, spent his entire life, actually, trying to be, of all things, a legitimate American writer. He considered himself to be a writer, but his writing career was pathetic, a noncareer; his own people ignored, rejected the art that he produced. No matter that *Yokohama, California* was a "first"; it might as well have been a "last." No one took him seriously; he died

as he lived—in obscurity. He gave of himself as a
committed artist; all through the camps and after he
continued to produce his literature. His literature is
Japanese-American; he was committed to his people,
he lived up to his people, he saw his people as the stuff
of great art. He took the responsibility of founding
and maintaining the tradition of Japanese-American
literature. Toshio Mori did not fail; others failed him.
Yokohama, California is the start, the heart. It has
endured. It has the power—as never before, or after.
Now where is the laughter?

There is a related lesson in "My Mother Stands on
Her Head." In this story, Ishimoto-san, an old-time
food peddler, hardly appears in person. His is a strong,
felt presence, nevertheless, and the action revolves
around him, and the resultant reactions of others.
Ishimoto-san makes sales door-to-door; he delivers.
He used to be a community necessity. Now, he has
trouble competing with Safeway, making ends meet.
The mother of the story, to the consternation of her
price-minded family, continues to give him her business. The family protests about being gypped, so the
mother confronts him about it.

What Ishimoto-san does next is very simple, direct,
natural, funny, and disarming: he laughs, "'Ho-ho-
ho-ho-ho,'" then proceeds to give the mother "two
bean cakes and a big head of cabbage," for free. Before
long, "Ishimoto-san began coming as before."

This little story is as large as life; it is another Mori
masterpiece, a literary masterpiece as brilliant as it is

subtle: it has the wisdom of a parable. This is no mere story about money, the nickel-and-dime of life; this is a lesson in humanity, an example of moral obligation, of mutual responsibility, mutual trust: the bargain of life works both ways. In the old days of community support, community values, the people used to say: "I *give* him my *trade*." The trade-off was worth its weight in gold; it meant personal service, personal delivery, personal trust, personal dignity, the give-and-take of true community: commerce, compassion, understanding, harmony. No wonder "Ishimoto-san began coming as before." Thanks to the efforts of both the mother and Ishimoto-san, and the unspoken understanding of the family, the community will continue to survive, intact. The community is the core. It can adapt.

The relevance of this story to now is obvious: What to do with this book? What is it worth?

From the "new age" perspective, *Yokohama, California* might be considered sentimental—all the old folks, kids, families visiting one another unannounced, and people sitting on porches, talking around kitchen tables, are rather unfashionable now. There is a difference, however, between tear-jerking and the natural flow of things. This is a book of *strong* sentiment, certainly, for it is *moving* literature. This is what it is to be alive: the very strength of humanity.

There is, certainly, a burnished glow to the book which simply reflects the actual atmosphere of the time, the way the people felt, saw, and lived. Not that the book is gilded with goodness from cover to cover; on the contrary, the people and incidents portrayed are very real, with more aspirations than outright successes. But there are no failures, no real losers and victims. This was, after all, a time of hope and optimism, of established communities, of flourishing culture, of the new generation getting on with America. This was a time of pride and accomplishment. The people quite obviously believed in themselves, in what they could do, were doing, in America.

This sense of pride, of tradition, of continuing and extending the tradition is the whole point of "Nodas in America." (As a matter of fact, this might be said to be the whole point of the book.) Thus, at the close of the story, a child has been born:

> "This is Annabelle," Mama Noda said, holding up the baby. "George's baby. "She's *sansei,* you know."
>
> "Third generation," I agreed.
>
> "Pretty soon fourth generation," she said, smiling.
>
> "*Shisei,*" I said, nodding my head; and we went into the living room.

This is the lineage. It counts. It means something, everything: the tradition, the heritage: Japanese America.

And if the people get sentimental about who they are, so be it—it's in the blood. Some folks are just prone to sentimentality; some folks get all stirred-up by singing songs like "Auld Lang Syne," "Danny Boy," and "Lift Every Voice and Sing." They take pride in who they are, in their "sentimental" people. Some folks have been known to cry about the passing of the buffalo. Or, as Big Joe Turner sings about the passing of his community in Kansas City: "I dreamed last night I was standing on Eighteenth and Vine; / Shook hands with Piney Brown—well, I just couldn't keep from crying." The story, "Lil' Yokohama," is a shining example of the atmosphere, the time: "In Lil' Yokohama, as the youngsters call our community, we have twenty-four hours every day . . . and morning, noon, and night roll on regularly just as in Boston, Cincinnati, Birmingham, Kansas City, Minneapolis, and Emeryville."

The story is not only an overview of "Yokohama" but of Japanese America—the interrelated communities. That's the way the people saw things—there just happened to be a bunch of other folks around. The "Great Northern California game is under way":

It was a splendid day to be out. The sun is warm, and in the stands the clerks, the grocers, the dentists, the doctors, the florists, the lawnmower-pushers, the housekeepers, the wives, the old men sun themselves and crack peanuts. Everybody in Lil' Yokohama is out. Papa Hatanaka, the father of baseball among California Japanese, is sitting in the stands behind the backstop, in the customary white shirt—coatless, hatless, brown as chocolate

and perspiring: great voice, great physique, great
lover of baseball.

The story continues to detail the events of the rest of
the week, after the game. (Interestingly enough, even
in those days of the color barrier, Toshio the ballplayer
was granted a tryout by the Chicago Cubs.) There is
young Ray Tatemoto being seen off at the train station, "leaving for New York, for the big city to study
journalism at Columbia. Everybody says he is taking a
chance going so far away from home and his folks." A
chance it is, and the chances are he will never be hired
to write for a "regular American" paper. No matter, for
the Japanese-American journalistic tradition is flourishing, including the first bilingual newspaper in
America.

The overview concludes in a revery of music and
sunlight, old folks on porches reading papers like the
Mainichi News, and kids coming home from a variety
of schools, learning, participating in the ways of the
land: "The day is here and is Lil' Yokohama's day." This
was the time known to every Japanese American as
"before the war." If anything, with the destruction of
communities, the story has become even more sentimental. Young Japanese Americans might even regard
a story like this with nostalgia—for the future.

"The Woman Who Makes Swell Doughnuts" might
very well be considered the most sentimental story in
the book. Actually, this might not even be considered
a story at all: it is static, uneventful, with no real plot

progression, no character development, no real conflict. In actuality, this work of fiction belongs in its own category: *tribute*. And conventional literary terminology is limited in application. Thus, to say that the story is sentimental is not appropriate, is not the entire story. Rather, it might be said the story captures and conveys those qualities known as *yasashi*—a known, a given, but practically untranslatable. To say that a person, a story, is *yasashi*, is considerable. These terms come to mind: humility, respect, sweetness, devotion, caring, generosity, kindness, and warmth— the very essence of strength and wisdom. The best of humanity.

This woman, then, is a source of sustenance and food for thought. She is a way of being, seeing ("'You will be glad later for everything you have done with all your might.'"), a philosophy, a way of life. No wonder Toshio devotes such time and care to this portrait, this tribute to an anonymous woman on Seventh Street: no wonder he wants to share his sense of this Mama, this grandmother, with the rest of the world: this is the mother of Japanese America. This is no mere story: this is an anthem.

The years have passed since then. "Yokohama" is no more; the woman in the story was surely put into the camps, starting with the Tanforan Race Track. It is no accident that when *Yokohama, California* finally was published, in 1949, the dedication read:

> *To the Memory of My Mother*
> *Yoshi Takaki Mori*

III. Style As Substance

Yokohama, California readily qualifies for greatness on literary merit alone. It meets all the standards. It has originality, excellence. It is a work of art. Toshio took himself seriously, as a serious writer, a man of letters working to develop his art, his craft, and his work must be regarded accordingly.

Thus, while his humble beginnings are the stuff of legend, it is the work that really matters. No matter that he had only a high school education—he educated himself, he read incessantly or as time from his jobs allowed, he haunted bookstores and libraries, and most of what he wrote he wrote after hours, at night. No matter, either, that he was an Oriental, an unheard of animal in the Occidental world of mainstream American literature. But whoever heard of a Japanese American fiction writer? And, who could take one seriously? That would mean that the man and his people were just as good as anybody else. Toshio Mori as good as Sinclair Lewis? Ridiculous.

This was back in the days when "colored" entertainers weren't considered legitimate artists. (The most famous and highly regarded "colored" writer of the time had to be Pearl S. Buck, who was awarded the Nobel Prize for Literature in 1938.) Toshio had to know the odds; he had a "Chinaman's chance" of making it as a writer particularly if he did not deliver what the public might have thought it wanted: Orientalia, exotica . . . He had his own vision, his own potential, and he meant to do something with it.

He studied French writers, Russian writers, and like most of his American contemporaries, he was an admirer of Sherwood Anderson. As critic Malcolm Cowley states in his introduction to Anderson's collection of stories, *Winesburg, Ohio:* Anderson is "the only story teller of his generation who left his mark on the style and vision of the generation that followed. Hemingway, Faulkner, Wolfe, Steinbeck, Caldwell, Saroyan, Henry Miller. . . ."

Toshio's name deserves to be on that list, and why his works are not included in standard collections of American literature says more about American values than the value of Toshio Mori. Toshio acknowledges Anderson in the very title of his own book—a gesture of respect, of tradition—and though he also utilizes Anderson's concept of a centralized location, Anderson's work serves mainly as a point of departure.

For one thing, Anderson's book, originally titled *The Book of The Grotesque,* and portraying, in Cowley's terms, "emotional cripples," is very much its own work—as "Yokohama" is very much its own entity and community, characterized by warmth and humor. Toshio's book is no mere mirror image, but an individual work with its own spirit and feeling. The story "Akira Yano" establishes the distance between Anderson and Mori. Akira is an aspiring, self-deluded writer very much in the Anderson vein; he produces, it seems, imitation Anderson. Thus, the narrator says, in a gentle way, "Akira Yano was miserable and I think his prose too, was miserable."

What really distinguishes Mori from Anderson, or from any other writer for that matter, is the writing itself. No other writer writes like Mori. He achieved what few writers ever achieve—the *mezurashi*—"the highly unusual"—an individual style. He developed his own voice, his own way with words; he became a master craftsman; he is an authentic original.

To test the Mori style as style, to judge its effectiveness, it would be quite simple to take any story and remove its Japanese names and terms, rendering it "generic." The story would lose something but it would still be an effective work of literature, with the style being seen for what it is: solid, functional. The stories seem to tell themselves—the mark of a master. The stories seem to grow from the inside out, naturally, organically, from seed to flower. There is subtlety, understatement and, when appropriate, long, stately passages flow and soar into music. Mori's style delivers. It is more innate than ornate. No flab, no waste. It is not style for style itself.

Yet style and substance are inextricable in Mori's work. Thus, to render a story "generic" is to remove an elemental essence. Japanese America is no mere flavor; it is a way of life, a lifestyle, a way of being, experiencing, perceiving, a holistic structure. In effect, Toshio Mori, the American writer, the stylist in English, developed and employed a Japanese-American typewriter.

No wonder, then, that there are no white people in all of *Yokohama, California.* Except for the possible exception of an on-stage blonde in the story, "Toshio Mori," everyone else is or could very well be Japanese American. This is not "reverse-racism" —for whites like Dewey, Lincoln, Emerson are mentioned in the same breath as Noguchi, Akegarasu, and Shak-yamuni. The point is, this is a Japanese-American community—the people do not define themselves as nonwhite, nor do they need to rely on whites. Whites are just there, like street names, like racism—they come with the territory. Japaneseness is also taken for granted. It is no big revelation that "The All-American Girl" ("'One of those frail beauties who makes history.'") goes by the name of Ayako Saito. Yokohama, California; Japanese, America—all that is regarded as fitting and natural.

This leads to what might be considered Toshio's most remarkable achievement. It is so remarkable as to be unnoticable. Most everyone of Toshio's generation was accused of having an accent. This came from being bilingual, from learning the home language first. For Toshio, this represented more *access* than handicap, for it enabled him to experience the greater world and to convey it through his stories. Surely, in many of the stories, the characters, especially the elders, are actually speaking Japanese, but Toshio has captured the nuances in plain and regular English.

This is not the stuff of stereotypes, of bogus dialects and translations. Instead, the reader is allowed to

experience the people and situations directly, immediately. In effect, Toshio allows each reader to *be* a
Japanese American and to experience that life, from
the inside out.

IV. History As Strategy

The rest is history. The publishing history of *Yokohama, California* is a story in itself; it spans the times.
It is both landmark and watershed, representative of
key periods in Japanese-American, American history:
before the war, the camps, after the war, and now,
whatever this period might be called, when there is
talk of redress and reparations, when a publisher like
the University of Washington Press has an entire line
of important Asian-American works.

It's all right here in the book: 1942, 1949, 1985 . . .
The book was written in the late 1930s and early 1940s
although some of the stories might take place in the
1920s or earlier. The book was accepted for publication in 1941, slated to be issued in 1942, finally
appeared in 1949, and went out of print.

The history is right here in these very pages, like
rings of a tree: Saroyan's initial Introduction, his
update, the dedication (Toshio's mother survived the
camps), and two stories that are an obvious addition to
an already intact manuscript. There are two versions of
the book, then—the "original" and the "additional."
The Caxton Printers apparently did the adding. Why?

The first additional story, "Tomorrow Is Coming, Children," also happens to be the leadoff story, the one that sets the tone for the book. It has a job to do, and it tries—it tries to introduce Japanese America, it tries to explain Japanese America as American. This approach was not necessary before the war, but someone deemed it crucial in 1949. Why?

It doesn't take much knowledge of history to come up with answers. For instance, what Saroyan said in his initial Introduction had an entirely different ring in 1949: "He is a young Japanese, born somewhere in California, and the first real Japanese-American writer. He writes about the Japanese of California. . . ." Despite the fact that Saroyan also said that "Toshio Mori is probably one of the most important new writers in the country at the moment," that didn't mean the same, or much, in 1949.

"A Jap's a Jap!"—that had been in all the papers. Everybody knew that. And, while before the war, people might have been moderately interested in a book by a Japanese American, an Oriental, a Nisei, even a Jap (the term was nothing new), by 1949, all this was something else indeed. It was as if, in the interim, Toshio, the "new writer," had become many different things—all variations of Jap. For instance, not even Nisei was a simple, domestic term; rather, with the outbreak of war, the government treated both Nisei and Issei as "enemy aliens" (like Toshio's mother who had been denied the rights to American citizenship). A Jap's a Jap, so the government, in effect, put the Constitution on hold, removed the "American" from Japanese American, and sent everybody to camp. (Toshio's brother was in the American Army before the war, so he stayed in the Army and suffered a debilitating injury in Europe—while his family was in the camps.)

In the camps, Toshio became, among other things, a government ward, an evacuee, an internee, a relocatee, a resident of Topaz Camp, Millard County, Utah. By 1949, he was simply a former this and that—of assembly centers, of evacuation camps, of concentration camps, of whatever, all under the jurisdiction of the War Relocation Authority, Department of the Interior—and there were some things that would be there forever: "When did you stop being a Jap?"

By 1949, as Toshio had become less than an author, the book had become less than literature—it was not to be read so much as inspected. It had been tarnished, not burnished, by time, and was lucky to have snuck into print the way it did. By its very nature, it was destined for obscurity; it had to be one of the most unwanted books in history. (Is it any wonder that Japanese America did not welcome this prose with its unprosaic subject matter and unprosaic title?)

The inclusion and placement of "Tomorrow Is Coming, Children," then, can be seen as Caxton's attempt to soften history, to start with bygones and get into the book in a positive way; the nondiscerning reader might even think that the bulk of the book takes place *after* the war, with the people having made a remarkable recovery. This story, however, does not fit, does not work. It belongs in another collection, in its own context, post-"Yokohama," for it was written in the camps, for a camp audience (including, of course, camp administration), and it was published not once but twice, in the same issue of the Topaz Camp magazine, *Trek,* in 1943—in English, and in Japanese translation. It's the featured piece (Toshio was not an editor of this issue), with illustrations.

Explanations, justifications, were the order of the day in camp; thus, the grandma of this story attempts to explain history to her grandkids, Annabelle and Johnny. She talks about leaving Japan, living in California, and how war has given her this "opportunity" to be in camp. She may not legally be a citizen but she feels very American—after all these kids and years— "I belong here." Besides, as she puts it, "Ah, San Francisco, my dream city. My San Francisco is everywhere."

Johnny doesn't comprehend these philosophical platitudes. He doesn't quite understand why war has gotten them into camp, instead of being back home "attending school with your neighborhood friends." He has difficulty with the "good points" of war, the "lessons," the "positive." Perhaps it's a bit like espousing American democracy behind barbed wire. So she sends the kids off to bed.

Now, on the surface, this seems to preach a pro-American message of perseverance. Sure enough, it's there, and should have satisfied the authorities (even though they may have wondered a bit about the translation). The *type* of perseverance being taught, however, is another matter. Grandma is not advocating amnesia, she is not saying "forget it," or "let bygones be bygones." As a matter of fact, all her reminiscence has a double edge to it, and the ironies had to be bouncing off the barracks, in two languages, for grandma, without saying it, is really saying: "*Remember*." Remember your uncle fighting overseas; remember this camp; remember me. Grandma is actually teaching history, interpretation, survival tactics, strategy—in the guise of a bedtime story. Pro-Japanese American, or pro-American, is not necessarily pro-white, or anti-Japanese. Another "sentimental" piece by Toshio Mori.

The other additional story goes by the name of "Slant-Eyed Americans." There are no "slant-eyes" in the rest of the collection, but here there are also "Nisei," "enemy aliens," "Japanese faces," "American," "American way of life," "true American," "Caucasian American," and "American citizen." (In the story "The Brothers," the term "American" is used to designate "generic" white, whereas "Japanese" is used to denote Japanese American.) This story, though not the end of the collection, signals the end of the community of "Yokohama." Yet it is not necessarily a Pearl Harbor story; rather, it is about community strength and family devotion. The younger son is home on leave from the Army: "Keep up the fire, that was his company's motto. It was evident that he was a soldier. He had gone beyond life and death matter, where true soldiers of war or peace must travel, and had returned." The story ends on an ominous note as the family sees him off to war: "We stood and watched until the last of the train was lost in the night of darkness." Before long, the family, too, will be gone from "Yokohama." The community will be no more.

V. Mori Territory

Mori territory is a world of freedom—freedom to be, to do, to try. Thus, the concluding story in the collection is about a plain woman who admires Clark Gable:

> When one has been around the neighborhood a while, the routine is familiar and is not emphasized. It appears dull and colorless. But in this routine there is the breath-taking suspense that is alive and enormous, although the outcome and prospect of it is a pretty obvious thing. Although her hope may be unfilled there is no reason why she cannot be a lover of Clark Gable.

This is the essence of Mori wisdom—to go for it, to go for broke, to believe. As the Mama of the doughnuts tells her grandchildren: "'I say to them, play, play hard, go out there and play hard. You will be glad later for everything you have done with all your might.'" In

so doing, a person enlarges and determines one's own
life. This is the perspective of a self-sufficient, self-
determining community.

Yokohama, California is full of such examples—of
people attempting, doing, acting; of committed people; of people making stands. The people live and
embody a philosophy. There is more to this book than
an old, anonymous woman, doughnuts, an old laundryman, an old grocer, a lonely writer, florists, clerks,
would-be writers, would-be financiers, kids playing,
men working, mothers worrying, eggs, laughing
faces, trees, pompons, movies with Clark Gable . . .
Mori territory is inclusive, incorporating—everywhere.

It is interesting to look at the Saroyan Introduction
in this light. The Introduction, by now, is a perma-
nent part of Yokohama, California, and it might be said
that Saroyan has assumed residency—as a Moriesque
character, "The Fresno Philosopher." The Introduction is no mere Introduction; it is Saroyan doing a
Saroyan. It is full of poses, postures, gestures, pro-
nouncements. It has darks, lights, louds, softs, starting with the long title and the tone of the first sen-
tence: "Of the thousand of unpublished writers in
America . . ." It has the feel of a sermon, a lecture. It
reveals a great deal, intentionally and not, about
Saroyan.

It is a very curious piece—original, worthy of
inclusion—but at the same time it is somewhat of a
nonintroduction. It has sides to it; it reveals much.

Saroyan is obviously being truthful about Mori (he admired Toshio's work; he sought him out; the men became friends; they had much in common—two California ethnic writers of modest beginnings), and though he has an introductory strategy, he doesn't stick to it. Instead, he succumbs to, resorts to, the inappropriate: overabundant Saroyanness; *sayonara,* Mori.

Consider this: Saroyan has arranged to introduce Toshio to a big-time book reviewer. This reviewer also has connections to a "New York publishing house," as does Saroyan. Saroyan is optimistic about Toshio's chances; after all, Saroyan, just two years Toshio's senior, had become an overnight sensation with the publication of a single book. While Toshio waits in the reception room, Saroyan goes in first: "I've got a writer I want you to meet. He'd flunk English, but he's a natural. He can't help it—but he's got to become more lucid. He's Japanese, writes about Japanese, but his characters are people first. I'll tell you—I don't know what's happened to me since I last saw you. I feel as if I've forfeited something. I mean, with all this recognition, or because of the acknowledgment, there's still a loneliness, but even that's not the same. I mean, I don't mean to confuse you, but it *is* confusing—all sorts of troubles, either way. By the way, here's his book."

The point is, Saroyan would probably never have introduced a "regular" writer this way— by "playing teacher." But Saroyan feels obliged to go public about this, because he is leading up to his concept of the "natural born writer"—one who "can't help" doing things on purpose by accident: "naturally." This implies the "primitive," as if Toshio is not a deliberate artist, and a highly sophisticated and innovative one at that. As it is, Toshio is presented as a limited, subliterary writer who must become more "lucid," whatever that may mean.

Saroyan, the unlettered ethnic, may very well have been subjected to this very same treatment. It is very easy to imagine this scenario: "Bill, you've got the goods, you're a natural but for god's sake we're going to have to do something about mechanics, aren't we. And, while we're at it, we'll help you become more lucid." The scenario continues: "Bill, even though you've got Armenians in your stories, well by god we think of them as people first—and the readers love 'em." Thus, Saroyan feels obliged to say that Toshio's characters "are Japanese only after you know they are men and women alive."

This is, of course, the old melting pot idea. In the guise of Americanization and universality, this was not so much acceptance but denial, domestication, and some folks were not about to melt down. A book like *Yokohama, California* is its best defense, its own integrity, and so be it if the characters are even *too* Japanese, this is its very strength.

No matter. Saroyan was simply reflecting the times; he was a free man. He didn't have to do anything; he could have ignored, abandoned Toshio, the way everyone else did. No matter, either, that in his 1948 update, Saroyan only said that the book "was postponed." He must have had his reasons, and Toshio's best interests in mind. Saroyan was a fine writer and a true friend; it is no accident that he contributed commentary to the first Japanese-American book of poetry. As Toshio might have said: "Anyone can do an introduction, but there is only one Saroyan."

There is only one Toshio Mori. There is only one *Yokohama, California*. We stand on Seventh Street. "I promise the reader a real experience in reading."

Lawson Fusao Inada

Ashland, Oregon
30 January 1985

Introduction to the Original Edition

AN INFORMAL INTRODUCTION TO THE SHORT
STORIES OF THE NEW AMERICAN WRITER FROM
CALIFORNIA, TOSHIO MORI.

OF THE THOUSANDS OF UNPUBLISHED WRITERS IN
America there are probably no more than three who
cannot write better English than Toshio Mori. His
stories are full of grammatical errors. His use of
English, especially when he is most eager to say something good, is very bad. Any high-school teacher of
English would flunk him in grammar and punctua-
tion.

In spite of all this, Toshio Mori is probably one of
the most important new writers in the country at the
moment.

He is a natural-born writer. At his best a natural-
born writer *does not* write with language. At his best
a writer who is not a natural-born writer *does* write
with language; he has no alternative. A natural-born
writer can't help saying something worth hearing.
Any other writer has to try very hard to do so.

It will be better for him when Toshio Mori learns
to be more lucid, but what he has already is what other
writers try for years to get, and sometimes never do.
I mean the Eye. He can see. He can see *through* the
material image to the real thing; through a human
being to the strange, comical, melancholy truth that

changes a fool to a great solemn hero. With the Eye he has also the Heart. The fine heart of the true writer. He has understanding, sympathy, generosity, and kindliness.

He is a young Japanese, born somewhere in California, and the first real Japanese-American writer. He writes about the Japanese of California. If someone else tried to tell you about them, you would never know them. Even if another young Japanese without Mori's Eye and Heart told about them, they wouldn't be what they are in Mori's little stories. They would be Japanese; in Mori's stories they are Japanese only after you know they are men and women alive.

I regard Toshio Mori as an important American writer. If he is never published by a New York publishing house, he will still be an important writer, but I feel sure it will not be long until he is published by a New York publishing house.

Writers are never discovered. They work hard for years, in loneliness nobody should misunderstand, and then finally somebody publishes one of their stories and the biggest change in the world begins to take place: the unpublished writer begins to forfeit the loneliness he has known, and which has nourished him, for the recognition he has, in loneliness, been working for. Except for the loneliness, he cannot ever have the recognition; except for the labor, he cannot have the ease, the smiling acknowledgment of the acknowledgment of his arrival. This loneliness is the same that all people know whose loneliness is not personal, the loneliness which is the most solemn part of all people, and the most comical. When this exchange begins to take place, the time is a tough one for the writer, even though pleasant.

I do not wish to be regarded as the discoverer of this young writer. I am delighted about his appearance, his arrival from the Japanese of California, but I am also a little embarrassed about writing these few words as an introduction to his work. I am embarrassed because I know how sincere and great his appreciation will be. The worst is yet to come for him. Two things can happen: he can succeed terribly and have new troubles of all kinds, between himself and the world and his writing; or he can make a beginning and not succeed and have other troubles of all kinds. In either event I know he will go on writing. If he succeeds, he will wonder about his writing, if it is truly what it should be; if he fails, he will wonder about it for other reasons, and have other kinds of troubles. Nothing can happen one way or another but it will make trouble, so that part of it is no matter. Mori's first story was published by *The Coast*, of San Francisco. I believe Christopher Rand uncovered the story, liked it, and helped edit it. It was called "The Brothers" and is in this little book.

Nobody can ever tell a writer what to do about his writing to make it better than it is. All I can do is hope that Toshio Mori will grow more lucid and at the same time not lose any of the things he has which belong to him alone. In the meantime his work in this book is young, fresh, innocent, somber, and full of comedy.

NOTE: The foregoing lines were written in San Francisco six or seven years ago. Publication of Toshio Mori's first book was postponed, but here it is at last, as fresh as ever. I promise the reader a real experience in reading.

WILLIAM SAROYAN.

New York
October, 1948

TO THE MEMORY OF MY MOTHER
YOSHI TAKAKI MORI

Acknowledgment is made to the following publications for their permission to reprint some of the stories in this book: *The Coast, Common Ground, Current Life, Pacific Citizen, New Directions, The Clipper, The Writer's Forum, Trek,* and *Matrix.*

Toshio working in the garden in the late forties. The San Leandro hills and the Mori nursery are in the background.

Table of Contents

	PAGE
TOMORROW IS COMING, CHILDREN	15
THE WOMAN WHO MAKES SWELL DOUGHNUTS	22
THE SEVENTH STREET PHILOSOPHER	26
MY MOTHER STANDS ON HER HEAD	33
TOSHIO MORI	39
THE END OF THE LINE	46
SAY IT WITH FLOWERS	54
AKIRA YANO	65
LIL' YOKOHAMA	71
THE FINANCE OVER AT DOI'S	77
THREE JAPANESE MOTHERS	84
THE ALL-AMERICAN GIRL	91
THE CHESSMEN	97
NODAS IN AMERICA	108
THE EGGS OF THE WORLD	115
HE WHO HAS THE LAUGHING FACE	121
SLANT-EYED AMERICANS	127
THE TREES	136
THE SIX ROWS OF POMPONS	140
BUSINESS AT ELEVEN	148
THE BROTHERS	155
TOMORROW AND TODAY	162

YOKOHAMA, CALIFORNIA

Tomorrow is Coming, Children

LONG AGO, CHILDREN, I LIVED IN A COUNTRY CALLED Japan. Your grandpa was already in California earning money for my boat ticket. The village people rarely went out of Japan and were shocked when they heard I was following your grandpa as soon as the money came.

"America!" they cried. "America is on the other side of the world! You will be in a strange country. You cannot read or write their language. What will you do?" I smiled, and in my dreams I saw the San Francisco your grandpa wrote about: San Francisco, the city with strange enticing food; the city with gold coins; the city with many strange faces and music; the city with great buildings and ships.

One day his letter came with the money. "Come at once," he wrote. "Don't delay." The neighbors rushed excitedly to the house. "Don't go! Live among us," they cried. "There will be war between America and Japan. You will be caught in mid-Pacific. You will never reach America." But I was determined. They painted the lonely lives of immigrants in a strange land. They cried on my shoulders and embraced me. "I have bought my ticket and my things are packed. I am going," I said.

For thirty days and nights the village people invited me to their houses, and I was dined and feted. It was hard not to change my mind and put off the trip.

They came to see me off at the station. They waved their hands cheerfully though their eyes were sad. But my spirits were not dampened. I was looking ahead, thinking of your grandpa and San Francisco.

My brother went with me to Kobe, and not until the boat was pulling away from the pier did I feel a pain in my breast. Yes, I cried. The first night I could not sleep. I kept hearing my friends' words: "Hurry back. We will be waiting. Remember us. . . . Best of health to you." The boat began to toss and we could not go up on deck. I grew seasick. What kind of a boat? Tiny, though at that time we thought it was big. The liners of today are three and four times as large. . . . Yes, your grandma is old. She is of the first generation. You children are of the third. . . .

The sea was rough and I was sick almost all the way. There were others in the room just as ill. I couldn't touch the food. I began to have crazy thoughts. Why was I going to America? Why had I been foolish enough to leave my village? For days I could not lift my head. Turn back? Did the ship turn back for me? No, child. A steamer never turns back for an individual. Not for death or birth or storm. No more does life.

Now your grandma is old. She will die some day just like your grandpa. Yes, child, I know, you love me. But when I pass away and the days roll by, you will find life goes on. How do I know? Just this morning Annabelle lost a quarter somewhere on the street. Her mama told her not to hold it in her hands but put it in her purse. No, she wanted her way and

lost it. That is experience, child. That is how I know.
I lost Grandpa. I lost my boy. I lost my mother and
father. Long ago I lost my friends in Japan. . . . Here,
I am rambling. . . .

When the boat finally passed the Golden Gate, I
had my first glimpse of San Francisco. I was on deck
for hours, waiting for the golden city of dreams. I
stood there with the other immigrants, chatting ner-
vously and excitedly. First we saw only a thin shore-
line. "America! America! We're in America!"
someone cried. Others took up the cry, and presently
the deck was full of eager faces. Finally we began to
see the dirty brown hills and the houses that jutted
out of the ground. This was different from what I
had dreamed, and I was speechless. I had expected to
see the green hills of Japan and the low sloping houses
duplicated here. No, child, it wasn't disappointment
exactly, but I had a lump in my throat. "This is San
Francisco. My San Francisco," I murmured to myself.

What was I wearing, Annabelle? My best kimono,
a beautiful thing. But do you know what your grandpa did when he saw me come off the boat? He looked
at it and shook his head. He hauled me around as if he
were ashamed of me. I could not understand.

"Never wear this thing again," he told me that
night.

"Why?" I demanded. "It is a beautiful kimono."

"You look like a foreigner," he said. "You must
dress like an American. You belong here."

He gave me a dress, a coat, a hat, stockings, and
shoes, my first American clothes. I stopped dozens of

times in front of the mirror to see how I looked. Yes,
I remember the big hats they used to wear then, and
the long skirts that dusted the dirt off the streets.
Some day I shall go up to the attic of our Oakland
home and bring down the album and show you the
pictures of those old days.

I cannot find the street now where your grandpa
and I lived that first year but it is somewhere in San
Francisco. We had a small empty house and no money.
We spread our blankets on the floor and slept. We
used big boxes for tables and small ones for chairs.
The city of my dreams began to frighten me. Rocks
were thrown at the house and the windows smashed
to bits. Loud cries and laughter followed each attack,
and I cowered in the corner waiting for the end.

"Oh, why did I come? Whatever did we come for?"
I asked your grandpa.

He only looked at me. "Just a little more time. . . .
a little more time," his eyes seemed to say.

I could not refuse. But we moved out of San Francisco. We came across the Bay, and after much saving
your grandpa bought a bathhouse in Oakland. And
that was where your daddy was born. We lived in the
rear, and for four years it was our home. Ah, the year
your daddy was born! That was when for the first
time I began to feel at home.

It was on account of a little neighbor, the white
American wife of a Japanese acrobat. They were
touring the country as headliners but had settled down
in Oakland for some reason. They lived next door
with their adopted Japanese children. "Mich-chan,

Taka-chan! Come home! Mich-chan, Taka-chan!"
Her cries used to ring across the yard like a caress.

The Japanese acrobat came often. "Please come and
talk with my American wife. She is lonely and has no
friend here," he told me.

I shook my head ashamedly. "I am lonely, too, but
I cannot speak English. When your American wife
starts talking, I am in trouble," I explained.

Then he would laugh and scold me. "Talk? You
don't have to talk. My wife will understand. Please
do not be afraid."

One day the American lady came, and we had tea.
We drank silently and smiled. All the time I was
hoping she would not begin talking. She liked my tea
and cakes, I could tell. She talked of simple things so
that I would grasp a little of it. She would pick up
her teacup and ask, "Satsuma? Satsuma, Japan?"

I would nod eagerly. "Yes, Satsuma."

She came often. Every time we sat silently, sipped
tea, and smiled. Every once in awhile her Japanese
husband came and thanked me. "She is happy. She
has a friend."

"I do not speak to her. I cannot express myself," I
told him.

"No, no. She understands. You do not have to talk."

Ah, I can never forget her. She knitted baby clothes
for your daddy. "I think it will be a girl," she said.
But it was your daddy. I cried when she had to go
away again. Yes, it was long ago. All your uncles and
aunts came afterwards: Mamoru, Yuri, Willie, Mary
Ann, Yoshio and Betty.

Yes, time is your friend in America, children. See, my face and hands are wrinkled, my hair gray. My teeth are gone, my figure bent. These are of America. I still cannot speak English too well, but I live among all kinds of people and come and go like the seasons, the bees, and the flowers. Ah, San Francisco, my dream city. My San Francisco is everywhere. I like the dirty brown hills, the black soil and the sandy beaches. I like the tall buildings, the bridges, the parks and the roar of city traffic. They are of me and I feel like humming.

You don't understand, Johnny? Ah, you are young. You will. Your grandma wants to be buried here in America. Yes, little ones. Once I had a brother and a sister in Japan. Long ago they wrote me a letter. Come back, sister, they said. We want to see you again. Hurry. Oh, it was long before you were born. But I did not return. I never saw them again. Now they are dead. I stayed in America; I belong here.

Now I do not ask myself: why did I come? The fog has lifted. Yes, Annabelle and Johnny, we are at war. I do not forget the fact. How can I ever forget? My mother country and my adopted land at war! Incredulous! After all these years when men of peace got along together. Your grandma sometimes cries in the night when her eyes open. No, not for herself. She is thinking of your Uncle Mamoru in the U.S. Infantry "somewhere" overseas and his comrades, and the people going through hardships and sufferings. In time of war, weak men fall and the strong triumph.

You will learn, little ones, that life is harsh at times.

War is painful. If there were no war we would not be in a relocation center. We would be back in our house on Market Street, hanging out our wash on the clothesline and watering our flower garden. You would be attending school with your neighborhood friends. Ah, war is terrifying. It upsets personal life and hopes. But war has its good points too.

In what way, Johnny? Well, you learn your lessons quickly during wartimes. You become positive. You cannot sit on the fence, you must choose sides. War has given your grandmother an opportunity to find where her heart lay. To her surprise her choice had been made long ago, and no war will sway her a bit. For grandma the sky is clear. The sun is shining.

But I am old. This where you come in. Children, you must grow big and useful. This is your world. . . .

Now run along to bed like a good boy and girl. Sleep and rise early. Tomorrow is coming, children.

The Woman Who Makes Swell Doughnuts

THERE IS NOTHING I LIKE TO DO BETTER THAN TO GO to her house and knock on the door and when she opens the door, to go in. It is one of the experiences I will long remember—perhaps the only immortality that I will ever be lucky to meet in my short life— and when I say experience I do not mean the actual movement, the motor of our lives. I mean by exper- ience the dancing of emotions before our eyes and inside of us, the dance that is still but is the roar and the force capable of stirring the earth and the people.

Of course, she, the woman I visit, is old and of her youthful beauty there is little left. Her face of today is coarse with hard water and there is no question that she has lived her life: given birth to six children, worked side by side with her man for forty years, working in the fields, working in the house, caring for the grandchildren, facing the summers and winters and also the springs and autumns, running the house- hold that is completely her little world. And when I came on the scene, when I discovered her in her little house on Seventh Street, all of her life was behind, all of her task in this world was tabbed, looked into, thoroughly attended, and all that is before her in life and the world, all that could be before her now was to sit and be served; duty done, work done, time clock punched; old-age pension or old-age security; easy chair; soft serene hours till death take her. But this was not of her, not the least bit of her.

When I visit her she takes me to the coziest chair in the living room, where are her magazines and books in Japanese and English. "Sit down," she says. "Make yourself comfortable. I will come back with some hot doughnuts just out of oil."

And before I can turn a page of a magazine she is back with a plateful of hot doughnuts. There is nothing I can do to describe her doughnuts; it is in class by itself, without words, without demonstration. It is a doughnut, just a plain doughnut just out of oil but it is different, unique. Perhaps when I am eating her doughnuts I am really eating her; I have this foolish notion in my head many times and whenever I catch myself doing so I say, that is not so, that is not true. Her doughnuts really taste swell, she is the best cook I have ever known, Oriental dishes or American dishes.

I bow humbly that such a room, such a house exists in my neighborhood so I may dash in and out when my spirit wanes, when hell is loose. I sing gratefully that such a simple and common experience becomes an event, an event of necessity and growth. It is an event that is a part of me, an addition to the elements of the earth, water, fire, and air, and I seek the day when it will become a part of everyone.

All her friends, old and young, call her Mama. Everybody calls her Mama. That is not new, it is logical. I suppose there is in every block of every city in America a woman who can be called Mama by her friends and the strangers meeting her. This is commonplace, it is not new and the old sentimentality may be the undoing of the moniker. But what of a woman who isn't a mama but is, and instead of priding in the expansion of her little world, takes her little circle, living out her days in the little circle, perhaps never to be exploited in a biography or on everybody's tongue, but enclosed, shut, excluded from world news and newsreels; just sitting, just moving, just alive, planting the plants in the fields, caring for the children and the grandchildren and baking the tastiest doughnuts this side of the next world.

When I sit with her I do not need to ask deep questions, I do not need to know Plato or The Sacred Books of the East or dancing. I do not need to be on guard. But I am on guard and foot-loose because the room is alive.

"Where are the grandchildren?" I say. "Where are Mickey, Tadao, and Yaeko?"

"They are out in the yard," she says. "I say to them, play, play hard, go out there and play hard. You will be glad later for everything you have done with all your might."

Sometimes we sit many minutes in silence. Silence does not bother her. She says silence is the most beautiful symphony, she says the air breathed in silence is sweeter and sadder. That is about all we talk of. Sometimes I sit and gaze out the window and watch the Southern Pacific trains rumble by and the vehicles whizz with speed. And sometimes she catches me doing this and she nods her head and I know she understands that I think the silence in the room is great, and also the roar and the dust of the outside is great, and when she is nodding I understand that she is saying that this, her little room, her little circle, is a depot, a pause, for the weary traveler, but outside, outside of her little world there is dissonance, hugeness of another kind, and the travel to do. So she has her little house, she bakes the grandest doughnuts, and inside of her she houses a little depot.

She is still alive, not dead in our hours, still at the old address on Seventh Street, and stopping the narrative here about her, about her most unique doughnuts, and about her personality, is the best piece of thinking I have ever done. By having her alive, by the prospect of seeing her many more times, I have many things to think and look for in the future. Most stories would end with her death, would wait till she is peacefully dead and peacefully at rest but I cannot wait that long. I think she will grow, and her hot doughnuts just out of the oil will grow with softness and touch. And I think it would be a shame to talk of her doughnuts after she is dead, after she is formless.

Instead I take today to talk of her and her wonderful doughnuts when the earth is something to her, when the people from all parts of the earth may drop in and taste the flavor, her flavor, which is everyone's and all flavor; talk to her, sit with her, and also taste the silence of her room and the silence that is herself; and finally go away to hope and keep alive what is alive in her, on earth and in men, expressly myself.

The Seventh Street Philosopher

HE IS WHAT OUR COMMUNITY CALLS THE SEVENTH
Street philosopher. This is because Motoji Tsunoda
used to live on Seventh Street sixteen or seventeen
years ago and loved even then to spout philosophy and
talk to the people. Today he is living on an estate of
an old lady who has hired him as a launderer for a
dozen years or so. Every once so often he comes out
of his washroom, out of obscurity, to mingle among
his people and this is usually the beginning of something like a furore, something that upsets the community, the people, and Motoji Tsunoda alike.

There is nothing like it in our community, nothing
so fruitless and irritable which lasts so long and per-
sists in making a show; only Motoji Tsunoda is unique.
Perhaps his being alone, a widower, working alone in
his sad washroom in the old lady's basement and washing the stuff that drops from the chute and drying
them on the line, has quite a bit to do with his behavior
when he meets the people of our community. Anyway
when Motoji Tsunoda comes to the town and enters
into the company of the evening all his silent hours
and silent vigils with deep thoughts and books come to
the fore and there is no stopping of his flow of words
and thoughts. Generally, the people are impolite when
Motoji Tsunoda begins speaking, and the company of
the evening either disperse quite early or entirely ig-
nore his philosophical thoughts and begin conversa-

tions on business or weather or how the friends are getting along these days. And the strangeness of it all is that Motoji Tsunoda is a very quiet man, sitting quietly in the corner, listening to others talk until the opportunity comes. Then he will suddenly become alive and the subject and all the subjects in the world become his and the company of the evening his audience.

When Motoji Tsunoda comes to the house he usually stays till one in the morning or longer if everybody in the family are polite about it or are sympathetic with him. Sometimes there is no subject for him to talk of, having talked himself out but this does not slow him up. Instead he will think for a moment and then begin on his favorite topic: What is there for the individual to do today? And listening to him, watching him gesture desperately to bring over a point, I am often carried away by this meek man who launders for an old lady on weekdays. Not by his deep thoughts or crazy thoughts but by what he is and what he is actually and desperately trying to put across to the people and the world.

"Tsunoda-san, what are you going to speak on tonight?" my mother says when our family and Motoji Tsunoda settle down in the living room.

"What do you want to hear?" Motoji Tsunoda answers. "Shall it be about Shakyamuni's boyhood or shall we continue where we left off last week and talk about Dewey?"

That is a start. With the beginning of words there is no stopping of Motoji Tsunoda, there is no misery in his voice nor in his stance at the time as he would certainly possess in the old washroom. His tone perks up, his body becomes straight, and in a way this slight meek man becomes magnificent, powerful, and even inspired. He is proud of his debates with the numerous Buddhist clergymen and when he is in a fine fettle he delves into the various debates he has had in the past for the sake of his friends. And no matter what is said or what has happened in the evening Motoji Tsunoda will finally end his oration or debate with something about the tradition and the blood flow of Shakyamuni, St. Shinran, Akegarasu, and Motoji Tsunoda. He is not joking when he says this. He is very serious. When anyone begins kidding about it, he will sadly gaze at the joker and shake his head.

About this time something happened in our town which Motoji Tsunoda to this day is very proud of. It was an event which has prolonged the life of Motoji Tsunoda, acting as a stimulant, that of broadcasting to the world in general the apology of being alive.

It began very simply, nothing of deliberation, nothing of vanity or pride but simply the eventual event coming as the phenomenon of chance. There was the talk about this time of Akegarasu, the great philosopher of Japan, coming to our town to give a lecture. He, Akegarasu, was touring America, lecturing and studying and visiting Emerson's grave, so there was a good prospect of having this great philosopher come to our community and lecture. And before anyone was wise to his move Motoji Tsunoda voluntarily wrote to Akegarasu, asking him to lecture on the night of July 14 since that was the date he had hired the hall. And before Motoji Tsunoda had received an answer he went about the town, saying the great philosopher was coming, that he was coming to lecture at the hall.

He came to our house breathless with the news. Someone asked him if he had received a letter of acceptance and Akegarasu had consented to come.

"No, but he will come," Motoji Tsunoda said. "He will come and lecture. Be sure of that."

For days he went about preparing for the big reception, forgetting his laundering, forgetting his meekness, working as much as four men to get the Asahi Auditorium in shape. For days ahead he had all the chairs lined up, capable of seating five hundred people. Then the word came to him that the great philosopher was already on his way to Seattle to embark for Japan. This left Motoji Tsunoda very flat, leaving him to the mercy of the people who did not miss the opportunity to laugh and taunt him.

"What can you do?" they said and laughed. "What can you do but talk?"

Motoji Tsunoda came to the house, looking crestfallen and dull. We could not cheer him up that night; not once could we lift him from misery. But the next evening, unexpectedly, he came running in the house, his eyes shining, his whole being alive and powerful. "Do you know what?" he said to us. "I have an idea! A great idea."

So he sat down and told us that instead of wasting the beautiful hall, all decorated and cleaned and ready for five hundred people to come and sit down, he,

Motoji Tsunoda would give a lecture. He said he had already phoned the two Japanese papers to play up his lecture and let the world know he is lecturing on July 14. He said for us to be sure to come. He said he had phoned all his friends and acquaintances and reporters to be sure to come. He said he was going home now to plan his lecture, he said this was his happiest moment of his life and wondered why he did not think of giving a lecture at the Asahi Auditorium before. And as he strode off to his home and to lecture plans, for a moment I believed he had outgrown the life of a launderer, outgrown the meekness and derision, outgrown the patheticness of it and the loneliness. And seeing him stride off with unknown power and unknown energy I firmly believed Motoji Tsunoda was on his own, a philosopher by rights, as all men are in action and thought a philosopher by rights.

We did not see Motoji Tsunoda for several days. However in the afternoon of July 14 he came running up our steps. "Tonight is the big night, everybody," he said. "Be sure to be there tonight. I speak on a topic of great importance."

"What's the time?" I said.

"The lecture is at eight," he said. "Be sure to come, everybody."

The night of July 14 was like any other night, memorable, fascinating, miserable; bringing together under a single darkness, one night of performance, of patience and the impatience of the world, the bravery of a single inhabitant and the untold braveries of all the inhabitants of the earth, crying and uncrying for salvation and crying just the same; beautiful gestures and miserable gestures coming and going; and the thoughts unexpressed and the dreams pursued to be expressed.

We were first to be seated and we sat in the front. Every now and then I looked back to see if the people were coming in. At eight-ten there were six of us in the audience. Motoji Tsunoda came on the platform and sat down and when he saw us he nodded his head. He sat alone up there, he was to introduce himself.

We sat an hour or more to see if some delay had caused the people to be late. Once Motoji Tsunoda came down and walked to the entrance to see if the people were coming in. At nine-eighteen Motoji Tsunoda stood up and introduced himself. Counting the two babies there were eleven of us in the audience.

When he began to speak on his topic of the evening, "The Apology of Living," his voice did not quiver though Motoji Tsunoda was unused to public speaking and I think that was wonderful. I do not believe he was aware of his audience when he began to speak, whether it was a large audience or a small one. And I think that also was wonderful.

Motoji Tsunoda addressed the audience for three full hours without intermission. He hardly even took time out to drink a glass of water. He stood before us and in his beautiful sad way, tried to make us understand as he understood; tried with every bit of finesse and deep thought to reveal to us the beautiful world he could see and marvel at, but which we could not see.

Then the lecture was over and Motoji Tsunoda sat

down and wiped his face. It was wonderful, the spectacle; the individual standing up and expressing himself, the earth, the eternity, and the audience listening and snoring, and the beautiful auditorium standing ready to accommodate more people.

As for Motoji Tsunoda's speech that is another matter. In a way, however, I thought he did some beautiful philosophizing that night. No matter what his words might have meant, no matter what gestures and what provoking issues he might have spoken in the past, there was this man, standing up and talking to the world, and also talking to vindicate himself to the people, trying as hard as he could so he would not be misunderstood. And as he faced the eleven people in the audience including the two babies, he did not look foolish, he was not just a bag of wind. Instead I am sure he had a reason to stand up and have courage and bravery to offset the ridicule, the nonsense, and the misunderstanding.

And as he finished his lecture there was something worth while for everyone to hear and see, not just for the eleven persons in the auditorium but for the people of the earth: that of his voice, his gestures, his sadness, his patheticness, his bravery, which are of common lot and something the people, the inhabitants of the earth, could understand, sympathize and remember for awhile.

My Mother Stands on Her Head

THIS WAS THE THIRTY-NINTH TIME IT HAPPENED. Our family sat at the kitchen table and did nothing but talk. In the morning Ishimoto-san, the food peddler, had come and left a bill of statement. "What's the matter with that man?" my father kept saying. Then his face became red. "Mama, don't buy from him again! Don't buy, that's all!"

"Eleven dollars and eighty-five cents! For what?" my brother said. "This is funny. Who does he think he is? What did we buy from him?"

"How do we know? He doesn't leave the sales tag when we buy," I said. "And when does he put down what we buy? I haven't seen him with a sales book."

"Don't buy anything from him. That'll settle it," my father said.

"He's got a fine memory. He goes home in the evening and writes down what we bought that day," my brother said.

We laughed although we were sore. Every time we bought half a dozen articles he'd forget to leave one or two things. If it wasn't the matches it was the eggs. If it wasn't the eggs it was the butter.

"Look here," my mother angrily said, showing us the latest statement. "Look at the seventeenth. That was last Wednesday. He forgot to leave the eggs that day. I clearly remember it because I needed them, and he's got eighty cents down here. I told him to leave a pound of butter, two soybean cakes, and one dozen eggs. When he forgets the eggs how could it be eighty cents?"

"Don't buy from him," my father said. "He couldn't charge us anything on that."

"Let's see," my brother said. "A pound of butter from him must cost about forty cents, and the two soybean cakes is ten cents. That's fifty cents, and the eggs must be thirty cents to make it eighty cents altogether."

"That's the way it goes every time," my mother said, furiously. "What fools we are."

"Tell him to knock off the thirty cents," my brother said.

"Let's see you convince him he forgot the eggs," I said. "He'll swear that he left the eggs last Wednesday. He'll clearly remember that he gave us the box with the two brown eggs."

"You can't beat his memory," my father said.

Every Monday, Wednesday, and Friday Ishimoto-san came around in his 1928 Model-A Ford. He brought vegetables and groceries and peddled them within the radius of fifty miles. My mother pitied him, remembering the old days when he had a prosperous grocery store on Seventh Street. She saw him go down the ladder of success until he had only the old route left for a living. Even the route wasn't on a paying basis. The customers suffered for it, and we paid outlandish prices for things which we could have bought cheaply at the neighborhood stores. My father always squawked when he saw the bill.

"Today at the Safeway we could have bought the number one grade salad oil for a dollar and a quarter," he moaned to Mother. "That's cheap. Look at Ishimoto-san's price. A dollar and seventy."

"He sells a bit high," my mother admitted. "You know, he must bring it out here. And he must live."

"And we must live," my father said. "Don't buy from him, Mama. Buy at the Safeway and save."

Mother shook her head. "I couldn't do that," she said. "He's been coming here for twenty years, and I couldn't do a thing like that as if it's nothing."

Father was now on the defensive. "When I used to go to the Oakland Free Market for groceries I always used to see him there. You know what that market is —a retail market. He buys his stuff there and brings it out here and sells at a profit. How do you like that?"

Mother shook her head with finality. She knew all about it. It was an old story. Our neighbors quit buying from Ishimoto-san long ago. They learned from a competitive grocer that Ishimoto-san often came into his store and bought articles at retail price to peddle in the out-of-town district. The news wrecked Ishimoto-san's business in our district. One by one the customers dropped him.

"We won't drop him," my mother said. "We'll continue buying from him, even if it's a little amount."

"At the Safeway," my father observed, "you could buy Salinas lettuce three for a nickel. And you buy an apple-size lettuce from him for a nickel apiece."

"They're bigger than an apple," Mother defended herself and Ishimoto-san.

Ishimoto-san came regularly to the house. He pestered my mother. If she didn't want carrots would she care for dry onions. If she didn't want a can of bamboo sprouts would she need a package of shredded shrimp. Some days he would stop on the way home and look up my mother. When he found her he'd look anxiously at her.

"Would you lend me a dollar, Mama?" he'd ask. "I had a flat, and I must get a tire patch and fix my spare."

"Business is bad," my mother would say. "My boy goes collecting on the old bills and nothing comes in. This is a bad year for nurseries."

She would then drop her work and go in the house for the money. "Put two dollars credit on the bill," she'd tell Ishimoto-san. And he would go away happy, his problem solved.

Then this thing happened. We were putting Ishimoto-san on trial for one month. The month was July, and every time we bought something we mentally noted it down.

"I think our July bill will be around six dollars. Anyway it won't be over seven dollars," Mother calculated. She added, looking wisely at Father, "If Ishimoto-san's figures matches ours, Papa, you'll have no kick coming."

"Don't buy from him and you'll have no worry like this," Father said. He looked up brightly. "If he overcharges us this time we'll quit buying from him."

"In that case we'll stop buying from him," Mother agreed.

We didn't have to wait long. Punctually Ishimoto-san left the statement on the first. At noon we pounced on the statement as if it was an important pronouncement. My brother glanced at the total amount and whistled. My mother became furious for the first time on Ishimoto-san's account. My father laughed.

"Eleven eighty-five!" my brother echoed, and whistled again.

"The brainless fool! What does he use his head for?" Mother fumed.

Father continued to laugh.

My brother looked up from Ishimoto-san's statement as if he had suddenly smelled a rotten odor. He looked at us and then turned again to the paper.

"What's the matter?" I asked. "Anything wrong?"

"Wait a minute," he said importantly. He kept adding the figures. Then he looked up, convinced. "Add those figures, Papa. See if the total is right."

"Is his addition wrong too?" I asked my brother.

"Wrong?" he said, half-chuckling. "That guy's added a dollar and forty-nine on the total, that's all."

"What!" Mother cried. "This is the end. We'll never buy from him again."

Father added again and again. My brother went to the corner where the old bills were kept.

"What's happened to him lately?" Mother wanted to know. "Is he loose in the head?"

From the corner my brother exclaimed, "Here's some more profit for Ishimoto-san on last month's bill."

Mother moaned.

"He made a dollar on nothing," my brother continued. "It should have been seven thirty-three and he's got it down eight thirty-three."

My father finished adding at last. "Don't buy any more!" he shouted. "Don't buy any more."

We all agreed.

"No more," Mother said solemnly.

On his next round we watched Ishimoto-san from the house while Mother went out to meet him with the bill. We watched him add several times. Finally he scratched his head. He burst out, "Ho-ho-ho-ho-ho." His sweat-stained derby went up and down with vibration.

When Mother came in the house she had with her two bean cakes and a big head of cabbage.

"Did you buy those, Mama?" Father demanded.

"No. He gave these to me," she said somewhat sadly.

"Remember, don't buy any more," Father warned us.

"We won't buy again," we said.

For several weeks we didn't buy a thing. Sometimes Mother waved him away. Sometimes I did it. Then one day Mother lost her fury, and the old habit overtook her. Ishimoto-san began coming as before.

Toshio Mori

IN THE LATE AFTERNOON HE BEGAN WANTING TO GO to the city. When the quitting time came he wanted very much to go to the city. All day the spell of bleakness and dullness witched him, and although the day was unusually warm and sunny he could not erase the spell. He wanted to do something, to do anything, to move, to get over the feeling that was disturbing him. He could think of nothing to do but go to the city, to crush and wipe out this ominous feeling of standing alone, walking alone, going alone, without a nod or a smile or caress or better, an understanding from someone.

Tonight Teruo boarded the bus, leaving behind what to him was sad and dark today, and looking forward, expectantly, hopefully, to the night and the city and the people to revive him, his spirit and the return of undivorced feeling toward the world, the people, the life. He was certain there was that quality in the city to reward him for his efforts. He would go to the friends, go to the girls' houses, go to the spots that would bring back the old days, and go to show if necessary, go everywhere, go to all the places and the people tonight to drown out this senseless strain and motion.

He sat, riding to the city, without a thought of the past which was this afternoon, deliberately forgetting, erasing the melancholia. Once he recalled the afternoon. Must you go tonight? his mother had said. Yes, I must go tonight, he had said. I must go no matter what else happens. And he meant it. Tonight he could not sit with the family and talk. Tonight he could not listen to the radio; he could not read. He could not, moreover, sit in silence like other nights, in constant wake of himself and the field he worked in the daytime. So he was doing right tonight. Something in the city would divert his attention or someone would see and understand the state he was in and would lend a hand. Everything would come out all right, he said to himself; everything must come out all right.

Teruo got off at Twelth and Clay and walked down a block and turned up Eleventh Street. He headed straight for Tsuyuko's home without much thought. Then walking closer to the house that was gay and lively, he could see her sitting in the living room reading or listening to the short wave program from Japan or playing those sad melancholy songs on the Japanese records. He could see her running up to him when the doorbell rings and cry, Oh, hello! Teruo. How glad I am to see you!

He was confident she was home. And nearing her home he could see the bright lighted living room and knew she was home. She would always be home. That was her nature, he thought. So when she opened the door and squealed in delight he was certain now everything would turn out right.

"Oh, hello! Teruo," she said. "How delightful! Do come in!"

But that was not all. There were two young men in the room. He recognized one of them as Haruo Aratani and the other he did not know and Tsuyuko introduced him. They sat down and the conversation which was interrupted by his entrance was resumed. And between laughters and talk Tsuyuko asked him how he was getting along these days. He said he was just so-so.

The moment Teruo sat down he knew the place was not for him. There was the same gaiety and liveliness in the room, the same Tsuyuko of other nights, but it was not the same. As he sat in the midst of laughter and lively chatter he felt he was out of it all, alone, alien, orphaned. The contrast he was playing in the room, helplessly coming, shook him and the longer he remained in the room, the more he thought of this and the helplessness of himself. He sat forty minutes thinking, still hoping that something might happen, that some little bit of a thing or a gesture or a movement would change the makeup of the room to something that would resurrect him but it did not come. He sat ill, stifling, wanting to move, to talk, and that something did not happen and he did not move. Teruo left early, Tsuyuko saw him off at the door and told him to come again real soon. When he crossed the street to the other side he saw Tsuyuko through the window, returning to the living room that was gaiety and laughter and two young men.

He began to walk rapidly with no mind as to where he was going. For blocks he could think of nothing else. She was not at fault. She really was herself and the two young men were blameless. There was nothing that had irritated him, no incident, no envy or jealousy to be furious about. It made him all the more sad and deserted.

Just tonight, he thought. If we had been alone together, just tonight, it might have been different. She might understand, she might only have smiled and listened and said nothing and it might have done a world of good for him. Just to have her close to him tonight, to understand him as he understood his state of feeling, would have been sufficient. That was all he would ask for. She could go with the two young men anytime, anywhere, all the other times and that was all right. She could go as she pleased and that was right. But tonight, he thought, tonight was different.

After walking blocks of city blocks he remembered the home on Sixth Street. He could go and see Yuri. He was in town; this was the time to see her. He would talk to her. She was serious and read books and she might understand. In time, by talking and listening he might find the way to the outlet and forget the emptiness of self and dullness of time. She could understand; yes, she could.

He quickened his pace. Already it was nine o'clock. He must hasten to catch Yuri home. When he knocked on the door the mother came out. She said Yuri went out early and would not be home till late but wouldn't he come in and have tea. He declined; and having left the steps and the sidewalks of her block, he turned once more toward the city.

He could think of nothing else to do. He did not

feel like going to a movie now. Through his head raced a number of names that were familiar. Names of his friends, names of his parents' intimates, and of special names, Bob, Tora, Kazumi, Sumio, Min, George. But the names did not come alive; he could think of nothing to do in the city, having now played his hunches and failed.

Reaching the town he went in Tabe Drug's soda fountain and sat and ordered a vanilla milkshake. Razzy, the soda jerker, remembered him and hailed. "How's the tricks?" he said. "Not so hot," Teruo said, "does the old gang still come in?" "Yes, you bet," Razzy said. "Tora, Sumio, Kazumi, Bob, Butch, Min, George." "Have they come in recently?" Teruo said. "No, not for quite awhile," the soda jerker said. That was all.

While he was sipping his milkshake Sumio and his woman came in. Sumio came over and both slapped each other's back. "How's the old boy?" Sumio said. "Fine," said Teruo, "how are you?" "Great," said Sumio. They talked for awhile about the old gang and the old days, and then Sumio went back to his table.

Five minutes later Teruo said goodbye and left.

He walked up Broadway toward the theatrical center thinking of going home now at nine forty-five. There was nothing to do but go home. All his efforts had failed, each effort making him more miserable and conscious of aloneness and sadness. He decided he might just as well go home and bury himself in the bed.

But approaching the theater, his eyes were attracted to the bright lights of its front, bright and cheery in illumination, suggesting hope and cheerfulness inside. He might as well, he thought, take a last fling for the night. So Teruo bought a ticket and went inside the Roosevelt Theater to see the vaudeville.

He remembered watching a comic with a little bit of an accordion and a big size accordion. With the little accordion he had a trick note that made a noise like a raspberry from a human mouth. Every once in awhile he would sound this note and the people laughed. He had a face like Harry Langdon or Lloyd Hamilton of the old silent pictures, looking pathetic and funny. He was trying to be funny and wasn't funny, and was funny for the lack of it. Then Teruo remembered a lovely blonde singing into the microphone in her throaty voice, of being away from the Ozarks, of wanting to go back there, of seeing her pappy and the smell of chicken dinner, and of the Ozarks calling her back. It made him sad and her beautiful face and innocence made it all the more tragic and agonizing that she, with her beauty, should sing such sad songs. He could stand it no more. When the vaudeville was over he walked out of the theater missing the double features.

When Teruo reached home the house was dark. It was dead still as if no one were occupying the house but himself coming home and occupying the place. But he knew his parents were sleeping inside and his brothers were also sleeping.

He sat on the edge of the bed, making little noise, and began undressing. He was aware that the night was almost over, that tonight was almost through with him. But he knew he was not through with the state of his feeling. Instead, tonight increased the fervor of sadness and loneliness, and for a long while Teruo did not shut off his light.

He was still up at two in the morning. He could hear the breathing of his mother sleeping in the next room, and on the other side of the wall he could hear his brother snoring. He sat, aware that no one knew him as he knew himself. He knew even Mother and his brother Hajime could not see his state of feeling; that no one in this world would see, and if seeing would not see, unable to understand and share his state of feeling that was accumulating and had been accumulating since birth.

The End of the Line

HE CAME TO SEE MY PARENTS ABOUT SASAKI WHO WAS leaving for Japan. As usual Yamada had taken several bottles of sake before leaving his house. His bright-red face glowed with good will to the world, but his eyes were troubled. "Ah, one more," he said, shaking his head. "Another friend gone. One more less."

"We aren't going to lose his friendship," my father persisted. "We'll correspond. Our letters'll speak. We aren't going to lose anything."

"The first year or so, yes," Yamada said sadly. "For one year or so we write every month. We feel happy and comforted. Then times change. One month becomes two months. Two months becomes six months. Six months become a year; a year into two years, and then no more. I know it. My friends, good old friends —all of them same."

"That's true, Yamada-san. That's true," my mother agreed. "All our old friends are dying off or going back to Japan. When we die we'll have no friends at our funeral."

"Sometimes I think we're the biggest fools," Yamada said. "We see others go away. We go to their funerals. One by one they go away, and we are left behind to die alone."

The three old friends looked at one another and understood. Sasaki, Yamada, and my parents came from the same village in Japan. Whenever they got together they talked of the old days. Now my mother sat dreamily.

"They say our village has changed completely. The old landmarks are gone," my mother said.

"Otake is a fine modern city now," Yamada said. "I never went back but I know everything's different."

"Yes," my mother said. "My brother died last year and I have no near relatives living. My close friends died long ago."

"Let's go back and visit the old village before we die," Yamada said to my father.

My father shrugged his shoulders. "What for? I don't know anybody back home. Who would recognize us? Do you think that our friends' grandsons will know us? Some of their fathers we don't know."

"We would be strangers," Yamada agreed. "They'll think we're foreigners."

"When I think of my age I realize my time is short," my mother said. "Our time is coming pretty quick."

Yamada shook his fingers triumphantly. "That's why I always say, drink. Drink and enjoy. Join your friends' company and enjoy life as you go along."

My mother smiled. "Tonight, Yamada-san, there is no sake in the house. I'm sorry, but it's the truth."

"Never mind, never mind," Yamada said, waving his hand. "If there's no sake then wine will do. If there's no wine then beer will be all right. If there's no beer then I'll have to get along without it. Don't fuss over it. I had a bottle or two tonight."

"I have beer," my mother said. She got up to get some.

"Let's go up to Lake Tahoe," Yamada said to my father. "Let's go there for several days."

"I don't know. We're pretty busy," my father said.

"You're always busy. Take time out," Yamada said.

My mother brought three bottles of beer. Yamada's eyes lighted up a little. He watched her fill up his glass.

"What shall we do about Sasaki?" he said. "Where shall we hold his farewell banquet?"

"Let's go to Asia Low," my father suggested. "That's a good place. But I don't know what the others will say."

"By the way, what happened to Gen-yan? Is he still in Otake?" asked my mother.

"Yes, whatever happened to him?" my father said.

"I clearly remember the day I left the village for good," my mother said. "On the way to the station I saw Gen-yan fighting with two boys. Oh, he was smart and mischievous."

"Gen-yan? Ah, Gen-yan," said Yamada, thinking. He brightened. "Yes, he died last year in Osaka. My nephew wrote me about his big funeral. He was rich and popular."

My father shook his head. "I cannot believe it. I cannot believe it. Gen-yan, the little rascal who liked to walk barefooted."

Yamada laughed. He helped himself with the beer. "That must've been forty years ago."

My father nodded.

"He died wearing a beard. He had two grandsons," Yamada said.

"It was like yesterday that I saw Gen-yan walking up the path, throwing rocks at the ripe pears," my mother said.

"What happened to Yone-yan, Kane-yan, and To-mo-yan? I don't hear about them," my father said.

"They're all dead with the exception of Kane-yan," Yamada said. "He's eighty-four this year, but his legs are useless. It's too bad about Tomo-yan."

"What about Tomo-yan?" my mother asked.

"Didn't you know?" Yamada said. "He lost all his property holdings, and died a broken man."

My father sighed. "He was a big landowner. He was prosperous when I left Hiroshima."

"Better to live long without money," my mother said.

Yamada's eyes twinkled. "Let's go to Lake Tahoe. Let's go right away."

"Is there a chance of Sasaki-san coming back to America?" my mother said to Yamada.

He shook his head. "No, not a chance. He must look after the family estate."

"Is Sasaki sailing on the twenty-fourth?" my father asked.

"Yes, on *Kamakura Maru*," Yamada said. "He's lucky. That's the latest luxury liner."

My father smiled proudly. "Nowadays the steerage is better than the old time first-class cabins."

"I came over on a ship that weighed only seven thousand tons," my mother said. "We were tossed many times in the Pacific."

"Yes, time marches on," Yamada said dreamily. "I

used to drive the Model-T Ford, and go everywhere
by myself. Now I cannot drive. It isn't just the new
type of cars I'm afraid of. It's the speed and the new
regulations—it's the times. I ride on the bus to Oakland nowadays."

"You have Sei-chan and Tora-chan to drive for
you," my mother said.

"Yes," Yamada said, "but I have come to like the
bus too. I go on the bus whenever I have some business
in Oakland. And riding on the bus I get some funny
impressions. Sometimes they stick in my mind and I
cannot forget."

"What sort of impressions?" my mother said, smiling. "Do you have your daydreams on the bus?"

"Maybe and maybe not," Yamada said. He took
hold of a new bottle and opened it carefully. He tilted
his glass and slowly poured. "I have one impression
that always comes to me when I board the Hayward-
bound bus in Oakland."

"No fairy tales," my father warned. "I don't like
them."

"Keep still, Papa," my mother said.

Yamada smiled. He poured himself another glass of
beer. "I get on with a bunch of people, and we take
our seats. We sit for awhile in the same sphere of a
moment and then one by one we get off at our destina-
tion, and we separate. Sometimes I get to talk to
someone who is friendly, but that is only a moment.
By the time I get off at the end of the line I am alone
with the driver, and when I do get off he too is gone."

"Does it get you?" my mother said.

"Often I get sick," Yamada said. "Sometimes I think I am going away alone. Sometimes I believe I am leaving the earth forever. Sometimes I have a feeling that I am stepping off to meet warm arms and happy greetings, but that's rare."

There was a moment of silence. My mother broke the spell.

"About Sasaki-san," she said, brightly. "Have you selected a gift for them?"

"No," Yamada said. "I don't know what to give."

"I'm going to get some clothes for the girls," my mother said.

"It must be late," Yamada said, rising. "What time is it?"

My father looked at the clock. "Our clock goes fast. It must be around one o'clock or later."

Yamada finished the bottle, standing. "I must go. It's getting late." He walked over to the door and hesitated.

"Let's go to Lake Tahoe," he said to my father. "Let's go next week."

"We're too busy. Maybe next year," my father said.

"Next year!" Yamada said. "Maybe there's no next year for us."

"Just a moment, Yamada-san," my mother said. "Our boy'll take you home. Wait a moment."

"No," he said. "I'll go home by bus."

"It isn't a bother," my mother said.

Yamada stood by the door holding the doorknob.

"Didn't you like the Yosemite trip we took last year?" he asked my father. "Didn't you like it at all?"

My mother laughed. "For a couple of weeks he talked of nothing but Yosemite."

"Let's go," Yamada said eagerly. "We could make it a short trip if you're busy."

My father laughed and shook his head. "First of all, let's get the Sasaki farewell dinner settled. Will you arrange it?"

"I'll take charge of it," Yamada said. He looked sad. "I must go now but I don't want to. I'd like to stay here and talk on."

"We'll meet again, Yamada," my father said. "I'm sleepy."

"I'm sleepy. I don't want to go," Yamada said.

My mother smiled and rose to her feet. "You must go now. You'll be tired and sleepy tomorrow morning. You know there's work tomorrow."

Yamada sighed. "Yes, you must sleep sometime but you can always sleep when there's nothing else to do." He opened the door. He looked out and turned back. "Oh, I aimed to ask you about it when I came in and forgot. Your neighbor's house was dark when I came by. Where did they go?"

"They moved out a week ago," my father said. "They went to San Diego."

"They're living with their relatives now," my mother informed him. "The mother died a month ago, you know. She had cancer on the breast."

"So it was. So it was," Yamada said. "Yes, I must go now."

"Our boy'll take you home," my mother said.

"Never mind. I'll take the bus," Yamada said. "I must get used to going off alone."

My parents walked to the door and the three said good night, and Yamada went out and closed the door.

Say It With Flowers

HE WAS A QUEER ONE TO COME TO THE SHOP AND ASK Mr. Sasaki for a job, but at the time I kept my mouth shut. There was something about this young man's appearance which I could not altogether harmonize with a job as a clerk in a flower shop. I was a delivery boy for Mr. Sasaki then. I had seen clerks come and go, and although they were of various sorts of temperaments and conducts, all of them had the technique of waiting on the customers or acquired one eventually. You could never tell about a new one, however, and to be on the safe side I said nothing and watched our boss readily take on this young man. Anyhow we were glad to have an extra hand.

Mr. Sasaki undoubtedly remembered last year's rush when Tommy, Mr Sasaki and I had to do everything and had our hands tied behind our backs for having so many things to do at one time. He wanted to be ready this time. "Another clerk and we'll be all set for any kind of business," he used to tell us. When Teruo came around looking for a job he got it, and Morning Glory Flower Shop was all set for the year as far as our boss was concerned.

When Teruo reported for work the following morning Mr. Sasaki left him in Tommy's hand. Tommy was our number one clerk for a long time.

"Tommy, teach him all you can," Mr. Sasaki said. "Teruo's going to be with us from now on."

"Sure," Tommy said.

"Tommy's a good florist. You watch and listen to him," the boss told the young man.

"All right, Mr. Sasaki," the young man said. He turned to us and said, "My name is Teruo." We shook hands.

We got to know one another pretty well after that. He was a quiet fellow with very little words for any-body, but his smile disarmed a person. We soon learned that he knew nothing about florist business. He could identify a rose when he saw one, and gardenias and carnations too; but other flowers and materials were new to him.

"You fellows teach me something about this busi-ness and I'll be grateful. I want to start from the bot-tom," Teruo said.

Tommy and I nodded. We were pretty sure by then he was all right. Tommy eagerly went about showing Teruo the florist game. Every morning for several days Tommy repeated the prices of the flowers for him. He told Teruo what to do on telephone orders. How to keep the greens fresh; how to make bouquets, corsages, and sprays. "You need a little more time to learn how to make big funeral pieces," Tommy said. "That'll come later."

In a couple of weeks Teruo was just as good a clerk as we had had in a long time. He was curious almost to a fault, and was a glutton for work. It was about this time our boss decided to move ahead his yearly business trip to Seattle. Undoubtedly he was satisfied with Teruo, and he knew we could get along without him for awhile. He went off and left Tommy in full charge.

During Mr. Sasaki's absence I was often in the shop helping Tommy and Teruo with the customers and the orders. One day when Teruo learned that I once worked in the nursery and had experience in flower-growing he became inquisitive.

"How do you tell when a flower is fresh or old?" he asked me. "I can't tell one from the other. All I do is follow your instructions and sell the ones you tell me to sell first, but I can't tell one from the other."

I laughed. "You don't need to know that, Teruo," I told him. "When the customers ask you whether the flowers are fresh, say yes firmly. Our flowers are always fresh, madam."

Teruo picked up a vase of carnations. "These flowers came in four oar five days ago, didn't they?"

"You're right. Five days ago," I said.

"How long will they keep if a customer bought them today?" Teruo asked.

"I guess in this weather they'll hold a day or two," I said.

"Then they're old," Teruo almost gasped. "Why, we have fresh ones that last a week or so in the shop."

"Sure, Teruo. And why should you worry about that?" Tommy said. "You talk right to the customers and they'll believe you. Our flowers are always fresh? You bet they are! Just came in a little while ago from the market."

Teruo looked at us calmly. "That's a hard thing to say when you know it isn't true."

"You've got to get it over with sooner or later," I told him. "Everybody has to do it. You too, unless you want to lose your job."

"I don't think I can say it convincingly again," Teruo said. "I must've said yes forty times already when I didn't know any better. It'll be harder next time."

"You've said it forty times already so why can't you say yes forty million times more? What's the difference? Remember, Teruo, it's your business to live," Tommy said.

"I don't like it," Teruo said.

"Do we like it? Do you think we're any different from you?" Tommy asked Teruo. "You're just a green kid. You don't know any better so I don't get sore, but you got to play the game when you're in it. You understand, don't you?"

Teruo nodded. For a moment he stood and looked curiously at us for the first time, and then went away to water the potted plants.

In the ensuing weeks we watched Teruo develop into a slick sales clerk, but for one thing. If a customer forgot to ask about the condition of the flowers Teruo did splendidly. But if someone should mention about the freshness of the flowers he wilted right in front of the customer's eyes. Sometimes he would sputter. On other occasions he would stand gaping speechless, without a comeback. Sometimes, looking embarrassedly at us, he would take the customer to the fresh flowers in the rear and complete the sale.

"Don't do that any more, Teruo," Tommy warned

him one afternoon after watching him repeatedly sell the fresh ones. "You know we got plenty of the old stuff in the front. We can't throw all that stuff away. First thing you know the boss'll start losing money and we'll all be thrown out."

"I wish I could sell like you," Teruo said. "Whenever they ask me, is this fresh? How long will it keep? I lose all sense about selling the stuff, and begin to think of the difference between the fresh and the old stuff. Then the trouble begins."

"Remember, the boss has to run the shop so he can keep it going," Tommy told him. "When he returns next week you better not let him see you touch the fresh flowers in the rear."

On the day Mr. Sasaki came back to the shop we saw something unusual. For the first time I watched Teruo sell old stuff to a customer. I heard the man plainly ask him if the flowers would keep good, and very clearly I heard Teruo reply, Yes, sir. These flowers'll keep good. I looked at Tommy, and he winked back. When Teruo came back to make it into a bouquet he looked as if he had just discovered a snail in his mouth. Mr. Sasaki came back to the rear and watched him make the bouquet. When Teruo went up front to complete the sale Mr. Sasaki looked at Tommy and nodded approvingly.

When I went out to the truck to make my last delivery for the day Teruo followed me. "Gee, I feel rotten," he said to me. "Those flowers I sold won't last longer than tomorrow. I feel lousy. I'm lousy. The people'll get to know my word pretty soon."

"Forget it," I said. "Quit worrying. What's the matter with you?"

"I'm lousy," he said, and went back to the store.

Then one early morning the inevitable happened. While Teruo was selling the fresh flowers in the back to a customer Mr. Sasaki came in quietly and watched the transaction. The boss didn't say anything at the time. All day Teruo looked sick. He didn't know whether to explain to the boss or shut up.

While Teruo was out to lunch Mr. Sasaki called us aside. "How long has this been going on?" he asked us. He was pretty sore.

"He's been doing it off and on. We told him to quit it," Tommy said. "He says he feels rotten selling the old flowers."

"Old flowers!" snorted Mr. Sasaki. "I'll tell him plenty when he comes back. Old flowers! Maybe you can call them old at the wholesale market but they're not old in a flower shop."

"He feels guilty fooling the customers," Tommy explained.

The boss laughed impatiently. "That's no reason for a businessman."

When Teruo came back he knew what was up. He looked at us for a moment and then went about cleaning the stems of the old flowers.

"Teruo," Mr. Sasaki called.

Teruo approached us as if steeled for an attack.

"You've been selling fresh flowers and leaving the old ones go to waste. I can't afford that, Teruo," Mr. Sasaki said. "Why don't you do as you're told? We all sell the flowers in the front. I tell you they're not old in a flower shop. Why can't you sell them?"

"I don't like it, Mr. Sasaki," Teruo said. "When the people ask me if they're fresh I hate to answer. I feel rotten after selling the old ones."

"Look here, Teruo," Mr. Sasaki said. "I don't want to fire you. You're a good boy, and I know you need a job, but you've got to be a good clerk here or you're going out. Do you get me?"

"I get you," Teruo said.

In the morning we were all at the shop early. I had an eight o'clock delivery, and the others had to rush with a big funeral order. Teruo was there early. "Hello," he greeted us cheerfully as we came in. He was unusually high-spirited, and I couldn't account for it. He was there before us and had already filled out the eight o'clock package for me.

He was almost through with the funeral frame, padding it with wet moss and covering all over with brake fern, when Tommy came in. When Mr. Sasaki arrived Teruo waved his hand and cheerfully went about gathering the flowers for the funeral piece. As he flitted here and there he seemed as if he had forgotten our presence, even the boss. He looked at each vase, sized up the flowers, and then cocked his head at the next one. He did this with great deliberation, as if he were the boss and the last word in the shop. That was all right, but when a customer soon after came in he swiftly attended him as if he owned all the flowers in the world. When the man asked Teruo if he was getting fresh flowers without batting an eye escorted the customer into the rear and eventually showed and sold the fresh ones. He did it with so much grace, dignity and swiftness that we stood around like his stooges. However, Mr. Sasaki went on with his work as if nothing had happened.

Along towards noon Teruo attended his second customer. He fairly ran to greet an old lady who wanted a cheap bouquet around fifty cents for a dinner table. This time he not only went back to the rear for the fresh ones but added three or four extras. To make it more irritating for the boss who was watching every move, Teruo used an extra lot of maidenhair because the old lady was appreciative of his art of making bouquets. Tommy and I watched the boss fuming inside of his office.

When the old lady went out of the shop Mr. Sasaki was furious. "You're a blockhead. You have no business sense. What are you doing here?" he said to Teruo. "Are you crazy?"

Teruo looked cheerful enough. "I'm not crazy, Mr. Sasaki," he said. "And I'm not dumb. I just like to do it that way, that's all."

The boss turned to Tommy and me. "That boy's a sap," he said. "He's got no head."

Teruo laughed and walked off to the front with a broom. Mr. Sasaki shook his head. "What's the matter with him? I can't understand him," he said.

While the boss was out to lunch Teruo went on a mad spree. He waited on three customers at one time, ignoring our presence. It was amazing how he did it. He hurriedly took one customer's order and had him write a birthday greeting for it; jumped to the second customer's side and persuaded her to buy roses because they were the freshest of the lot. She wanted them delivered so he jotted the address down on the sales book, and leaped to the third customer.

"I want to buy that orchid in the window," she stated without deliberation.

"Do you have to have orchid, madam?"

"No," she said. "But I want something nice for tonight's ball, and I think the orchid will match my dress. Why do you ask?"

"If I were you I wouldn't buy that orchid," he told her. "It won't keep. I could sell it to you and make profit but I don't want to do that and spoil your evening. Come to the back, madam, and I'll show you some of the nicest gardenias in the market today. We call them Belmont and they're fresh today."

He came to the rear with the lady. We watched him pick out three of the biggest gardenias and make it into a corsage. When the lady went out with her package a little boy about eleven years old came in and wanted a twenty-five cent bouquet for his mother's birthday. Teruo waited on the boy. He was out in the front, and we saw him pick out a dozen of the two dollar-a-dozen roses and give them to the kid.

Tommy nudged me. "If he was the boss he couldn't do those things," he said.

"In the first place," I said, "I don't think he could be a boss."

"What do you think?" Tommy said. "Is he crazy? Is he trying to get himself fired?"

"I don't know," I said.

When Mr. Sasaki returned Teruo was waiting on another customer, a young lady.

"Did Teruo eat yet?" Mr. Sasaki asked Tommy.

"No, he won't go. He says he's not hungry today," Tommy said.

We watched Teruo talking to the young lady. The boss shook his head. Then it came. Teruo came back to the rear and picked out a dozen of the very fresh white roses and took them out to the lady.

"Aren't they lovely!" we heard her exclaim.

We watched him come back, take down a box, place several maidenhairs and asparagus, place the roses neatly inside, sprinkle a few drops, and then give it to her. We watched him thank her, and we noticed her smile and thanks. The girl walked out.

Mr. Sasaki ran excitedly to the front. "Teruo! She forgot to pay!"

Teruo stopped the boss on the way out. "Wait, Mr. Sasaki," he said. "I gave it to her."

"What!" the boss cried indignantly.

"She came in just to look around and see the flowers. She likes pretty roses. Don't you think she's wonderful?"

"What's the matter with you?" the boss said. "Are you crazy? What did she buy?"

"Nothing, I tell you," Teruo said. "I gave it to her because she admired it, and she's pretty enough to deserve beautiful things, and I liked her."

"You're fired! Get out!" Mr. Sasaki spluttered. "Don't come back to the store again."

"And I gave her fresh ones too," Teruo said.

Mr. Sasaki rolled out several bills from his pocket-book. "Here's your wages for this week. Now get out," he said.

"I don't want it," Teruo said. "You keep it and buy some more flowers."

"Here, take it. Get out," Mr. Sasaki said.

Teruo took the bills and rang up the cash register. "All right, I'll go now. I feel fine. I'm happy. Thanks to you." He waved his hand to Mr. Sasaki. "No hard feelings."

On the way out Teruo remembered our presence. He looked back. "Good-bye. Good luck," he said cheerfully to Tommy and me.

He walked out of the shop with his shoulders straight, head high, and whistling. He did not come back to see us again.

Akira Yano

WHEN I KNOCK ON THE DOOR AND ENTER HIS ROOM
he is usually sitting on the bed reading. The time I
visit is usually late and there is no time to lose. So
immediately we begin talking about what we have
done since the last meeting. This was a fine thing to
do, for Akira Yano and for myself, because this was
one way to keep company in those days.

Akira Yano came to the city from the valley. He
came principally to study, to become an electrical
engineer, but as I knew him he was a writer of prose.
He wrote more than he studied engineering, I thought.
Each time we met we talked about prose.

Not many people, not even the boarders in the same
house, knew anything about Akira Yano's love for
prose. This was not strange. Outside of Akira Yano's
family, I believe I was the only one who knew. Akira
Yano did not go around telling the folks he was a
writer. I guess he thought there was no sense in telling
anyone he was a prose writer because he was still
unpublished.

We became friends in a peculiar way. I knocked on
his door looking for a person whose name I forget.
And when Akira Yano came to the door I knew he was
the wrong person. But as he stood by the doorway I
saw he was holding Sherwood Anderson's *Winesburg,
Ohio*, so I cocked my head to one side to make sure,
and he saw me doing this.

"Do you like Sherwood Anderson?" he said.

"Yes. Very much," I said.

That was the beginning. We began to talk and pretty soon it was night. I learned then and there he was a writer of prose, unpublished. He learned I read modern literature. Since then we have seen each other countless times. Each time we met it was the same. He would talk about prose. And I would sit and listen to everything he said and knew about prose.

"Don't you study engineering any more?" I said.

"Sure, I do," he said. "Ah, but prose! There is something I can never tire of."

Some days he would show me his journal. Some days he would show me the sketches. One day he showed me a short story called, "The Eighty Days Through The Second Story Window." I thought it was fairly good but at worst it could be tripe. However, there were several passages in the story that gave hint of talent. Akira Yano thought it was his best piece so far. He said he would try the *Atlantic Monthly* or the *Scribner's*.

Nothing did come of it. In those days nothing would happen. It was not in the book, I guess, for anything to happen. We sat around and talked. The *Atlantic* and the *Scribner's* rejected the story. Akira Yano was miserable and I think his prose too, was miserable. We kept company quite often then and I knew he was sad and lonely and frustrated. Often I saw him go for days without touching an engineering book and I was certain his mind was blank as far as engineering was concerned.

"I don't know what's wrong with my prose," he said to me. "I am writing life, life as it is."

"I hope you will be in print real soon," I said.

That fall Akira Yano failed in the engineering course. His parents were shocked. From the valley the father wrote a long letter. He wrote, I am sending my son through college with my money so he may become an engineer. Remember, he is in the city to study engineering. Quit this nonsense, don't write any more stories. I don't want prose. If he cannot become an engineer, come home.

"What are you going to do, Akira?" I said.

"I cannot quit writing and I cannot disappoint Father so I will write and study too," he said.

For a week or so Akira Yano remembered his word. I saw him carrying around several engineering books. And on his table were several engineering problems he had worked out on the paper. However, before the finals for the term came around, the prose again was on his mind. Several weeks later Akira Yano was dropped from the college. And simultaneously, Akira Yano's father wrote a short letter.

Come home, he said, come home right away and become a farmer.

"What are you going to do?" I said.

"I guess I have to go home," Akira Yano said. "I have no money."

We corresponded after that. He wrote always about prose. I am free these days to write prose, he said. It is a great feeling. I have nothing to bother me. I write without worry. I think I am improving.

Several days later he would write again. I am writing more beautifully than ever, he said. I have written two stories; they are good. You should read them.

And again. You should read the story I wrote today, he said. It is almost perfect. It should be in O'Brien's collection of best short stories.

A month later he came to our house. He had several grips with him. "What are you doing with those suitcases?" I said. "Are you staying over?"

"I quit farming for good," Akira Yano said. "I cannot stand the valley heat. Farm work is too hard for me. I cannot stand that either."

"Are you staying in the city for good?" I said.

"Yes," he said, "I have come to stay for good. I will show Father what I can do with prose. I will climb to the top; there is no stopping me now."

So Akira Yano returned to the old boarding room. It was like the old days. I began to see him in the evenings. "How are you progressing, Akira?" I said.

"Today I wrote a story," he said. "And I wrote another yesterday. I have sent them out to *Harpers* this afternoon."

For about a month I kept going to his room every night. He wrote in the afternoons. In the evenings he sat on the bed reading and waited for me.

"I got another rejection today," he said to me one night. "It's the sixth one I've got this week."

"Perhaps a check will come for you one of these days," I said.

But the check did not come. The stories kept coming back and one night when I was later than usual

Akira Yano was not sitting on the bed reading and waiting for me. When I went in he was packing his suitcases.

"I must go to New York," he said. "I cannot sit cooped up here and rot away. I will get nowhere staying here. I must go to New York to be noticed."

"Have you the money to go and remain in New York?" I said.

"I am going to see Mother in the morning. I am sure she will help me," he said.

A month later I had a letter from Akira Yano in New York. He said he had already gone to see several publishers. He was going to collect his short stories and make a book. He said several publishers were very enthusiastic about the idea. Meanwhile, he said, he was staying at the Y.M.C.A. and writing stories for his second book which will be a greater book.

One day in spring I received an autographed copy of Akira Yano's *The Miserable Young Man*. Sixteen stories were included in the book. Some of them I recognized immediately, the stories which were rejected by the *Atlantic Monthly* and the *Scribner's* while he was still at the boardinghouse. Also, "The Eighty Days Through The Second Story Window" was included. Several days after the book came Akira Yano wrote me. He said he was very happy the book was so neat and handsome. He said he had paid three hundred dollars to have the book published. And didn't I think it was worth every penny of it? He went on to say that the book will appeal to the literary people, and also, by this week every big newspaper in

America will receive a copy and most likely, review it. He said he was very happy.

A little later another letter came from him. He said he was sending extra copies of the book to me so I may pass them around to the friends. He said he was doing splendid. He was writing beautiful prose for his second book. He will climb higher and make his presence felt in the world.

I watched the *Chronicle,* the *Examiner,* the *Tribune,* the *Post-Enquirer,* the *News,* to see if Akira Yano's book was reviewed. It was not reviewed nor was it once mentioned.

Sometime ago Akira Yano wrote again from New York. I have signed a contract with a major publishing company, he said. They are very impressed with my prose. My book will be out in a few months.

That was the last I heard from him. Perhaps I will hear from him again real soon. I don't know. Anyway, it is several years since he wrote to me about having signed up with a major book publishing company in New York.

Lil' Yokohama

IN LIL' YOKOHAMA, AS THE YOUNGSTERS CALL OUR community, we have twenty-four hours every day ... and morning, noon, and night roll on regularly just as in Boston, Cincinnati, Birmingham, Kansas City, Minneapolis, and Emeryville.

When the sun is out, the housewives sit on the porch or walk around the yard, puttering with this and that, and the old men who are in the house when it is cloudy or raining come out on the porch or sit in the shade and read the newspaper. The day is hot. All right, they like it. The day is cold. All right, all right. The people of Lil' Yokohama are here. *Here, here,* they cry with their presence just as the youngsters when the teachers call the roll. And when the people among people are sometimes missing from Lil' Yokohama's roll, perhaps forever, it is another matter; but the news belongs here just as does the weather.

Today young and old are at the Alameda ball grounds to see the big game: Alameda Taiiku *vs.* San Jose Asahis. The great Northern California game is under way. Will Slugger Hironaka hit that southpaw from San Jose? Will the same southpaw make the Alameda sluggers stand on their heads? It's the great question.

The popcorn man is doing big business. The day is hot. Everything is all set for a perfect day at the ball park. Everything is here, no matter what the outcome may be. The outcome of the game and the outcome of the day do not matter. Like the outcome of all things, the game and the day in Lil' Yokohama have little to do with this business of outcome. That is left for moralists to work on years later.

Meanwhile, here is the third inning. Boy, oh boy! The southpaw from San Jose, Sets Mizutani, has his old soupbone working. In three innings Alameda hasn't touched him, not even Slugger Hironaka. Along with Mizutani's airtight pitching, San Jose has managed to put across a run in the second. The San Jose fans cackle and cheer. "Atta-boy! Atta-boy!" The stands are a bustle of life, never still, noisy from by-talk and cries and the shouts and jeers and cheers from across the diamond. "Come on, Hironaka! Do your stuff!" ... "Wake up, Alameda! Blast the Asahis out of the park!" ... "Keep it up, Mizutani! This is your day! Tell 'em to watch the smoke go by." ... "Come on, Slugger! We want a homer! We want a homer!"

It was a splendid day to be out. The sun is warm, and in the stands the clerks, the grocers, the dentists, the doctors, the florists, the lawnmower-pushers, the housekeepers, the wives, the old men sun themselves and crack peanuts. Everybody in Lil' Yokohama is out. Papa Hatanaka, the father of baseball among California Japanese, is sitting in the stands behind the backstop, in the customary white shirt—coatless, hatless, brown as chocolate and perspiring: great voice, great physique, great lover of baseball. Mrs. Horita is here, the mother of Ted Horita, the star left fielder of

Alameda. Mr. and Mrs. Matsuda of Lil' Yokohama;
the Tatsunos; the families of Nodas, Uyedas, Abes,
Kikuchi, Yamanotos, Sasakis; Bob Fukuyama; Mike
Matoi; Mr. Tanaka, of Tanaka Hotel; Jane Miyazaki;
Hideo Mitoma; the Iriki sisters; Yuriko Tsudama;
Suda-san, Eto-san, Higuchi-san of our block, . . . the
faces we know but not the names: the names we know
and do not name.

In the seventh, Slugger Hironaka connects for a
home run with two on! The Alameda fans go mad.
They are still three runs behind, but what of that?
The game is young; the game is theirs till the last man
is out. But Mizutani is smoking them in today. Ten
strike-outs to his credit already.

The big game ends, and the San Jose Asahis win.
The score doesn't matter. Cheers and shouts and
laughter still ring in the stands. Finally it all ends—
the noise, the game, the life in the park; and the popcorn man starts his car and goes up Clement.

It is Sunday evening in Lil' Yokohama, and the late
dinners commence. Someone who did not go to the
game asks, "Who won today?" "San Jose," we say.
"Oh, gee," he says. "But Slugger knocked another
home run," we say. "What again? He sure is good!"
he says. "Big league scouts ought to size him up."
"Sure," we say.

Tomorrow is a school day, tomorrow is a work day,
tomorrow is another twenty-four hours. In Lil' Yokohama night is almost over. On Sunday nights the
block is peaceful and quiet. At eleven thirty-six Mr.

Komai dies of heart failure. For several days he has been in bed. For fourteen years he has lived on our block and done gardening work around Piedmont, Oakland, and San Leandro. His wife is left with five children. The neighbors go to the house to comfort the family and assist in the funeral preparations.

Today which is Monday the sun is bright again, but the sick cannot come out and enjoy it. Mrs. Koike is laid up with pneumonia and her friends are worried. She is well known in Lil' Yokohama.

Down the block a third-generation Japanese American is born. A boy. They name him Franklin Susumu Amano. The father does not know of the birth of his boy. He is out of town driving a truck for a grocer.

Sam Suda, who lives down the street with his mother, is opening a big fruit market in Oakland next week. For several years he has been in Los Angeles learning the ropes in the market business. Now he is ready to open one and hire a dozen or more men.

Upstairs in his little boarding room, the country boy has his paints and canvas ready before him. All his life Yukio Takaki has wanted to come to the city and become an artist. Now he is here; he lives on Seventh Street. He looks down from his window, and the vastness and complexity of life bewilder him. But he is happy. Why not? He may succeed or not in his ambition; that is not really important.

Sixteen days away, Satoru Ugaki and Tayeko Akagawa are to be married. Lil' Yokohama knows them well. Sam Suda is a good friend of Satoru Ugaki. The young Amanos know them. The Higuchis of our block are close friends of Tayeko Akagawa and her family.

Something is happening to the Etos of the block. All of a sudden they turn in their old '30 Chevrolet for a new Oldsmobile Eight! They follow this with a new living-room set and a radio and a new coat of paint for the house. On Sundays the whole family goes for an outing. Sometimes it is to Fleishhacker Pool or to Santa Cruz. It may be to Golden Gate Park or to the ocean or to their relatives in the country. . . . They did not strike oil or win the sweepstakes. Nothing of the kind happens in Lil' Yokohama, though it may any day. . . . What then?

Today which is Tuesday Lil' Yokohama is getting ready to see Ray Tatemoto off. He is leaving for New York, for the big city to study journalism at Columbia. Everybody says he is taking a chance going so far away from home and his folks. The air is a bit cool and cloudy. At the station Ray is nervous and grins foolishly. His friends bunch around him, shake hands, and wish him luck. This is his first trip out of the state. Now and then he looks at his watch and up and down the tracks to see if his train is coming.

When the train arrives and Ray Tatemoto is at last off for New York, we ride back on the cars to Lil' Yokohama. Well, Ray Tatemoto is gone, we say. The folks will not see him for four or six years. Perhaps never. Who can tell? We settle back in the seats and pretty soon we see the old buildings of Lil' Yokohama. We know we are home. . . . So it goes.

Today which is Wednesday we read in the *Mainichi*

News about the big games scheduled this Sunday. The San Jose Asahis will travel to Stockton to face the Yamatos. The Stockton fans want to see the champs play once again. At Alameda, the Sacramento Mikados will cross bats with the Taiiku Kai boys.

And today which is every day the sun is out again. The housewives sit on the porch and the old men sit in the shade and read the papers. Across the yard a radio goes full blast with Benny Goodman's band. The children come back from Lincoln Grammar School. In a little while the older ones will be returning from Tech High and McClymonds High. Young boys and young girls will go down the street together. The old folks from the porches and the windows will watch them go by and shake their heads and smile.

The day is here and is Lil' Yokohama's day.

The Finance Over at Doi's

EVERY TIME I VISIT SATORU DOI'S PLACE THERE IS
something doing, something new for me to listen to,
so every now and then I drop in at his house off
Seventh on Harrison Street to see what is going on in
the financial world, at the New York Stock Exchange
and at the San Francisco Stock Exchange and else-
where. This is where immediately, my friend, Satoru
Doi takes command of things, and I am led to a seat;
the minute he begins talking I sit mute and awed by
this little man's enthusiasm, his spirit and fire as he
tells me what has happened since the last visit.

"My boy, you are losing money every day!" he says.
"Now is the time to plunge! Don't waste a minute.
Look here!"

Then he thrusts out today's paper, the financial
section, to me. It is like this each time I drop in, only
sometimes with equal fire and enthusiasm he tells me,
hold the money, hold the cash, and just look at the
stock range today.

Over in the corner of the living room he has a stack
of financial sections cut out from the papers. When
the papers arrive at his house this is his first duty—
to cut out the financial section. He also subscribes
to the *Financial World* and has even taken a trial sub-
scription to the *Wall Street Journal.* I suppose this is
all a natural thing for a man interested in Wall Street
to do. I suppose the one who wishes to push ahead must

do this, putting his heart and soul into it, littering the living room and not giving a damn, losing the decency to live the normal life of the neighborhood, and always studying the daily prices of the market, burying his nose into it, giving all he has in mentality to probe the way to success in Wall Street. I do not know any other Wall Street men but this Satoru Doi I know, who is my friend and still living off Seventh on Harrison Street, often neglecting his shoe-repair business, and working wholeheartedly on the stock market.

This was early in 1937, the day when I went over to Satoru Doi's quite early. He was, as usual, sitting in the living room, poring over the statistics. Only this time I learned that he was looking over the old stock range. When he saw me at the door he leaped to his feet.

"You have come at the right time!" he cried. "Come in, come in."

"What are you excited about?" I asked.

"Sit down, sit down," he said. "This is no talk while standing."

"What is this all about?" I said. "Did you make some money in stocks?"

"No," he said. "But just as good. Do you k ̫ow what? Do you know that I would have cleaned up $314,786 if I had played with real money?"

"What do you mean?" I said.

"Look here, look here," he said. He shoved into my hands a 1933 financial section. "See these red pencil marks? See how I marked them in 1933 as if I had bought them at the time?"

"Yes," I said. "So you bought them."

"Yes, I didn't have any money at the time," he said, "but I bought them. I put these red marks down in 1933 as if I had bought them at the time. I wanted to see how I would come out."

"Gosh," I said. "So you would be $300,000 richer today!"

"That's the idea," Satoru Doi said, his eyes shining. He looked as if he wanted to hug me for understanding him, for listening to his great and secret achievement.

"I don't want you to think I am not on the level," he said. "I am not kidding you. I am telling the truth."

"I believe you all right," I said.

"Look here," he said, pointing at the 1933 stock list. "Look. I bought Warner Bros. at 1. I bought U.S. Steel at 23⅝, Republic Steel at 4, and Eastman Kodak at 47."

"You dropped one," I said. "You bought General Motors at 10."

"Oh yes," he said. "And there's another one, Transamerica at 2⅝. I honestly bought these at the time."

"Sure, I believe you," I said. "I think you're a financial wizard."

"Thanks," he said. He carefully put away the 1933 list.

"How much capital did you have in mind at the time?" I asked.

"About $10,000," Satoru Doi said.

"Too bad you didn't have the cash," I said.

"Next time I'll clean up," he said. He meant it. He looked fierce; he looked capable of doing anything, doing the impossible.

"I hope you will clean up a million," I said.

"Thanks," he said. "I know I will."

When I said I had to go home for supper he would not hear of it. His wife had the supper ready, he said, and I must eat. So I sat down with Satoru Doi and his family and had a simple beef stew and a plate of Japanese pickles.

When I went to see him again a month or two later he could not sit still to tell me the good news. He had bought 500 shares of Kinner Air at 19c and sold them at 27c. "I made about $40 on the transaction!"

"Good for you," I said.

"Next time I will go for a bigger game," he said. "I have my eyes on one stock that I know will make money."

"Do you mind telling me what it is?" I said.

"No, not at all," he said. "In fact I want you to get in on it. I have my eyes on Consolidated Textile. It is at 1 now but as soon as it falls to $\frac{7}{8}$ I am buying."

"Is it a good buy?" I asked.

"It is a good buy at 1," Satoru Doi said. "But if it drops to $\frac{7}{8}$ it's a still better buy."

When I saw him again it was at the butcher shop. He was purchasing a soup bone and ten cents worth of sausages.

"Do you know?" he said. "I am scrimping every penny these days. I will have enough saved up in two months to buy Consolidated, even at 1."

Two months later Satoru Doi did buy Consolidated Textile. He came to the house to tell me the news. He said he bought 300 shares of CTX at ⅞, and was he all set! The fall of 1937 and the year 1938 would be a great period of business boom.

"You watch," he said. "Everything is going up—materials, food, wages, and everything. Now is the time to plunge!"

"I hope you will clean up," I said.

Since then I have been looking into the financial section of *Tribune* to look up the Consolidated Textile and see how it had fared for the day. When the name Consolidated comes up I would start thinking of Satoru Doi in his shoe repair shop tacking on leather soles and thinking of Wall Street.

I watched the Consolidated hold ⅞ for a while and then fall successively to ¾, ⅝, and ½. One day it rallied to ⅝. Next day it fell again to ½, and then to ⅜, and finally down to ¼. The figures made Satoru Doi look so bad that I did not have the heart to visit him. I stayed away for several months.

One day Satoru Doi came to the house. He wanted to know if I could lend him a hundred, that he was in a hole, that he had food bills, the gas and electric, and the house rent to settle. I told him I wish I could help; I would gladly if I could but there was no money, and that I also could use some money.

He said that was all right; he had in mind to sell CTX at any price. Satoru Doi went away asking me to come and see him, saying that he wanted to show me the stocks he had marked in red as if he had bought them. He said that I should be in from the beginning so I would know there is no fake about the big profits in stocks.

Several days later I went to see him. He was sitting in the living room with several financial sheets scattered about, poring over this one and that one.

"Hello, hello," he cried. "Come over here. I want to show you something."

"What is it?" I asked.

"If I only had several thousand dollars!" he said. He showed me the stock range. "Look, I am marking them again as if I have bought them. See, I have bought Warner Bros. at 4, Paramount at 5⅛, Transamerica at 8, General Motors at 27½, and U.S. Steel at 42. And look what they are now, today."

Then he showed me the day's paper. He had the same red pencil mark underlying the stocks he had purchased. There were about ten or eleven stocks that were red-lined.

"You are cleaning up this time," I said. "By the way, what did you do with the Consolidated?"

"I sold it at ¼. I got a little over $40," he said. "I am going to save up again. This time I will clean up. You watch and see."

He sat there among the stacks of financial papers, his face shining with the fierce look that is characteristic of him, the capable-looking face that could accomplish the impossible but did not and could not, having failed thus far. I wondered then and there if there would be anything like a change in his little world or in Satoru Doi which would reconstruct his life of pathetic hope and miserable failures, help him to regain some kind of respect for himself and the dignity that is deserving to the living.

Three Japanese Mothers

IN WASHINGTON TOWNSHIP THERE ARE THREE WO-
men who are unique. They are unique in several
ways. As young girls they came over together in a
small steamer from a tiny village of Hiroshima prefecture some thirty years ago. They settled down in
the same community, raised families, and chose the
nursery life. With their husbands they raised flowers
for the city market. At first they experimented with
several kinds of flowers, roses, chrysanthemums, sweet
peas, and gardenias, but finally each of the three women and their husbands decided carnation growing
was most profitable and since then remained unchanged.

Their social circle is identical. Their duties in the
nursery and at home are pretty much the same. They
have the same thought of hitting the crops at Christmas and Mother's Day; they like to think of their
children as brilliant; and each of them would much
like to improve their stations in life. But this isn't
unique. It comes to the fore only when you begin to
notice them individually and see how they differ and
are human, and this is where I come in with a little bit
of their intimacies.

Every once so often the three women get together
at one of their homes and talk of things in general.
They talk about their husbands and the children. They
inform each other of the latest happenings of their

community. They talk about the crop and the progress of their plants. When they happen to run out of subjects one of them is certain to recall their girlhood days in Japan. Then their chats continue until one of the husbands calls to his wife or the noon whistle blows or something equally urgent pulls them apart.

When a Japanese woman reaches the age of sixty or thereabouts she becomes not so much concerned of her age but on how to conduct herself proper to her years and environment. Until her early fifties she may have a strong hope of attaining the womanly charm that was so characteristic in her youth. She may at this stage still do up her hair in the latest styles and follow other trends with equal interest. She may even be a bit foolish. But as soon as she reaches sixty or so her foolishness is gone. She is certain to become more practical and all the more conscious of her little world.

The three women who had been friends so long are no different from the people of their age. They are practical and what they see and do is always sane although Kiku, the oldest of the group, may be called impractical from one point of view which is unique.

There is one thing which the age did not spoil. They have retained their speech and are capable of outtalking the younger women. They could gain entrance to a conversation and dominate for the rest of the duration. It is when three of them get together and each lets down a little to hear the other side of it when it becomes as near a fifty-fifty proposition all around as possible. Such a time was Tane's oldest son's wedding day.

It was a home wedding and guests from all parts of the county were invited. The friends of the bride's and the groom's families came early expecting elaborate dinner and plenty of sake. They were not disappointed. Sake flowed freely and special dishes like *osashimi* and *osushi* were crammed for space on the tables. While the general guests were fêting the newlywed couple the three women were up in Tane's room. Once they came downstairs to see Tane's son and his bride off for their honeymoon. That done they were presently up in Tane's room.

"That's over," Tane sighed, and smiled contentedly at her friends.

"You are lucky, Tane," Tomi, the youngest of the three, said. "He is the last of your children safely married and you have no more worries. I still have my daughter to think of."

"Yes, I'm lucky," Tane said. "No more worries. No more hard work. Let the young take hold of old folks' burden."

"That is how I would like to be," Tomi said.

"You have no worry, Tomi," Tane said. "You have wealth. You have health. Your family life is amiable. What more do you need?"

"I have to account for my daughter," Tomi said.

"She'll be married in a year," Tane assured.

"Oh, she will," Kiku added.

Tomi confided to her friends, "When she is settled my husband and I are going to Japan to see my parents. Do you know how old they are now? My father is eighty-seven and Mother is eighty-four."

"Oh, you could go any time and anywhere," Kiku laughed. "You need not wait."

"Very true. That's true, Tomi," Tane said. "Look at us. My family is debt-ridden. Today my son is married. Do we wait till we are rich? Do we wait for a problem to be solved? No. My husband and I will take things easy now. My son knows we are leaving him many debts. Our place is heavily mortgaged and we pay principal and interest to the bank. We have lived our lives. Let them take over the budget accordingly. Let them worry about the much-used soil and the rotting greenhouses. That's the younger generation's problem."

"Oh, we don't coddle our children," Tomi said. "Our son wants more land and a new greenhouse, but we say no. You run our nursery in a profitable way and you can build a house easily, we tell him. I know we will spend more money for our journey to Japan than a piece of land and a greenhouse put together, but why should we miss our enjoyments when we know we have little time to live?"

"Certainly!" Tane agreed. "The young have lots of opportunities to see and do what they want."

"And how is your family these days, Kiku?" Tomi asked the one who had spoken only now and then. "I caught a glimpse of your second son here today."

Kiku smiled. "My children are healthy but insignificant," she said.

"No, no! You should praise them sky-high," protested Tane. "They're ambitious, frugal, and brilliant. Not like my boy."

"Your second son needs a bride," Tomi said. Kiku nodded her head. "He runs the nursery very efficiently," Tomi continued. "An excellent grower."

"He's made several mistakes last year but this year he's getting along," Kiku said.

"He doesn't need your help any more. You should rest often," Tomi said. "You work too hard."

Kiku smiled. She glanced at her two friends but said nothing.

"Kiku, how is your oldest son getting along?" asked Tane. "How many children has he now?"

"Three," Kiku said. "And another is coming in four months."

"I envy you," Tomi said. "You have three grandchildren already but you look younger than us. You work like a young ambitious matron and look it. I envy you."

"And your third son who is going to be a doctor?" Tane asked. "How long must he study yet?"

"Three more years," Kiku said. "I hope to live till he becomes a doctor."

Tomi and Tane sighed. "You lucky woman," they said.

On the way home sitting beside her second son who drove the car Kiku thought to herself, "I am a fool. I am a gentle fool sacrificing myself for the children. I don't have to but I do."

She looked at her second son who must have a bride in a year or so. "Money," she said pointedly. "We must make money to do anything."

Kiku recalled the chat with her friends in Tane's

room. "My friends are the lucky ones," she thought to herself. "They have ease, enjoyment, and no worry. They believe I work for the love of it. Even if I kneeled before the Buddha and swore I was the pillar of our family my friends wouldn't believe me. They'll gasp with surprise if they come to know my first son's vegetable market is failing. They don't know I am furnishing money or the creditors would attach his place."

Her second son took his eyes off the road for a moment. "Mother," he said, "we must make money this year."

"Yes, Son," Kiku said. "We'll make some this year."

Kiku looked at her son as he fell into silence. "Poor boy," she said to herself, "you'll have to wait awhile."

When their house loomed ahead Kiku saw the familiar light in the front room. Her third son who is to be a doctor was still up with his books. Her face lighted up with hope and her eyes sparkled a bit as she wished she could hurry into the house. She sighed with relief that the wedding was over and that her old dress had been passable at the gathering and she had not bought a new one. She remembered now that she could put that ten dollars she left on the bureau in the bank for the day when the third son was to open his office.

As the car neared the gate Kiku sat impatiently, wanting to run into the house and recapture the situation of her family's life. She looked at her second son, and her face showed little of the depression that had possessed her at the start of her ride. She looked at the dark clouds forming in the west. "Remember, Son," she said, "you must spray the plants before it rains. You mustn't let it go this time. Do it the first thing in the morning."

"All right, Mother," the son said.

"Tell Joe in the morning to start disbudding the red carnations in the number three house."

"All right," the son said. "I'll tell him."

She glanced at the dark skies and wished the rain would not come so soon. She sighed again as her thoughts returned to herself.

"I must be born a fool," she thought to herself. "A big fool because I cannot help myself for what I am." But she said it without pity, and the thought did not erase the eagerness nor the plans for tomorrow.

The All-American Girl

WE CALL HER THE ALL-AMERICAN GIRL, MY BROTHER and I. My brother started calling her that one day. We used to sit on the front porch of our house in the city and every once so often she used to walk past our house. We did not know her name. We watched her walk by, looking neither side, just walking in her trim little way. She walked by in a manner as if she was not aware of us, and possibly that was the beginning of the rub.

"There's a beauty," Hajime said one day when she passed. "Isn't she a beauty?"

"I don't know. I guess so," I said. It was the first time I had noticed her.

"She is a beauty," he said. "One of those frail beauties who makes history."

After that we could not help but notice her. She was like most Japanese girls, small, not more than five feet high. Unlike the girls of her size who are lively, restless, and energetic, her tininess made her look all the more frail.

"Here comes the beauty," Hajime said when she came down the street. "An All-American if there ever was one."

"Do you think so?" I said.

"Don't you think so?" he said.

I did not say anything. I did not know. One moment she looked frail and ordinary. The next moment she looked frail and extraordinary. She continued to pass the house. Each time she passed my brother commented. "She is the All-American Girl." He said it over and over. "Look how she carries herself," he said one day. "I wish I could put her on paper." He was going to an art school to be an artist. But he did not sketch her. We sat and watched her walk down the street.

One day she came by the house accompanied by another girl. They walked gaily and we heard her laugh and talk. We saw her face in smiles as she went by. The next day she came by the house again, this time alone. Her face which was laughter and talk and smiles was gone, and we saw her frail face again. Something is going on here, I said to myself, something is happening.

"What are you thinking about?" my brother said laughingly.

"The All-American was here," I said.

"You say it almost naturally," he said and laughed.

After that we both called her All-American. She came by the house almost regularly. We sat on the front porch and watched her go by. We did not speak to her but we knew she was aware of us and she knew we were aware of her. Once, Hajime wanted to run after her, stop her, and introduce ourselves.

"Let's know her," he said. "Let's get a tumble."

I did not say anything. We sat and did not move and the girl walked out of sight. After awhile I said, "Let us stay out of this. This is beautiful. Let it stay beautiful."

We sat and for the rest of the day did not see her again. Hajime sat beside me with a sketch pad on his knees and every once in awhile when someone passing caught his fancy he sketched in the figure with a pencil.

"Why don't you sketch the All-American?" I said.

"She cannot be sketched briefly," my brother said. "She must be given time."

"Why don't you take your time and do her face?" I said.

"I cannot paint her with time," he said. "I wish I could paint her now, today, but I cannot paint her."

"Her eyes are brown and they are round and big. Her hair is black and it is soft in natural curls and is bobbed. Her ears are always covered by her hair. Her lips are full and her nose is small. Her face is pale, only to flush when excited," I said.

"You must have seen her real close," he said. "Only I cannot paint her. Could you put her on paper?"

"No," I said, "not to do her justice."

One day we sat and waited for her on the porch. She came late in the afternoon. When she came in sight Hajime stopped sketching. When she passed the house he said, "She must come from a well-to-do home. Her clothes are of finest materials."

There was a time when I sat alone on the porch all day. Hajime was unusually late returning from the art class. The day was cloudy. I had been noticing this all afternoon and just as I looked up for the thirteenth or fourteenth time I found myself gazing into the All-American Girl's face and she was smiling. A moment later she was gone. I looked at her till she turned the block and disappeared. Beautiful, beautiful, I thought. When Hajime finally returned from school I told him how the All-American Girl came into vision and smiled and was gone. My brother laughed.

"You must have been dreaming this afternoon."

"No, no," I said. "She came five-thirty in the afternoon. She was wearing her yellow dress."

Next day Hajime and I were together again on the porch. She came quite early that day and when she saw us, she smiled. We smiled back and the moment was soon over and she was gone. "This is beautiful. Beautiful," Hajime said. "No words, no gestures. Nothing dramatic but all the drama in the world."

"We shall see," I said.

"She's ours. Our All-American Girl," Hajime said.

"Yes," I said, "but she does not know she is an All American to us."

"No," he said.

After that whenever she saw us she smiled. We said hello and greetings became quite the thing. But it never went beyond that.

"Shouldn't we go through with the adventure?" Hajime said to me. "All this is beautiful, yes. All this beauty is the halfway mark. Shouldn't we go through with this and see the ugly that is human?"

"No, Hajime. This once," I said, "let's sit and watch the beautiful. Let's have something beautiful to cling to without the ugliness."

"All right," he said. "We do not know her and she is beautiful."

"If something should happen now it would be beautiful all around," I said. "Something like life itself or circumstances breaking into our company."

"That would be beautiful," he said.

Something did happen several weeks later.

We sat for days on thé front porch without seeing her. Hajime wanted to know why this unusual thing was happening. "She will be coming along," I said. Then one day in the *Mainichi News* we saw her picture and the announcement of her marriage to a promising doctor in Los Angeles. It was the answer to her absence on our street. We learned her name for the first time. "Her name was Ayako Saito. That is our All-American Girl," Hajime said. "We will never see her again unless we are lucky."

"She was beautiful," I said.

We sat on the front steps and watched the sun go down beyond the rooftops and the trees.

"Our play is over," Hajime said.

"Do you think so?" I said.

"Perhaps it isn't over," he said.

We did not quit porch sitting. We sat all day, day in and day out. "The play isn't over," Hajime said to me one day. He had with him the paints and the brushes. He stopped attending the art class. We sat on the front porch and watched the traffic come and go. We watched the people walk by the house. Every now and then Hajime picked up his brush and painted.

We did not see the All-American Girl again. We sat on the front porch for a good many months. We were quite sure no girl we saw ever struck the note that the All-American Girl accomplished with her smile, departure, and mystery. We continued to sit on the front porch. We sat silent. Everything was before us, the whole world in fact, but we could not forget her.

One day Hajime said to me, "We must move on too. Our play isn't over." We agreed.

My brother picked up his paints and brushes again, and once more my eyes returned to see the traffic.

The Chessmen

PERHAPS I WOULD HAVE HEARD THE NEWS IN TIME, but if I hadn't met the third party of the three principals at the beginning it wouldn't have been the same to me. By luck that day, while I was leaning on the fence resting after a hot day's work, a young Japanese came up to me. "Hello. Where's Hatayama's nursery?" he asked me. "I was told the place was somewhere around here."

"It's half a mile farther down," I said. I pointed out the road and told him to go until he reached the greenhouses. That was Hatayama Nursery. The young Japanese thanked me and went away.

At Hatayama Nursery I knew two men, Hatayama-san and Nakagawa-san. They were the only men there the year around. The boss and his help. The two managed the three greenhouses of carnations quite capably. Only in the summer months when the carnation boxes must be lined up and filled with new soil and the plants for the next year planted, Hatayama-san hired additional men. Hatayama-Nakagawa combination worked beautifully. For seven years the two men never quarreled and seldom argued with each other. While Hatayama-san was at the flower market selling flowers to the florists Nakagawa-san carried on at the nursery. He was wise on everything. He attended the boiler, watered the plants, made cuttings, cut flowers and tackled the rest of the nursery work.

Every once in awhile I used to visit the place and talk to these middle-aged men. Perhaps Nakagawa-san was older than his boss. I don't know. "Listen to him, Takeo," Hatayama-san used to tell me. "If you want to become a good carnation grower listen to this man. He's got something. He has many years of experience and a young man like you will learn plenty by listening to him."

Nakagawa-san used to smile with these words. He talked very little. "I don't know much," he would say. "I know very little."

One of the strange things about Nakagawa-san was his family life. I used to visit him only on the weekdays. On Saturday nights and Sundays he was in Oakland to see his family. I used to wonder how he could stand it. His wife and three grown children lived in the city while he worked alone in the nursery. He made his bed, washed his work clothes, swept and mopped his bunkhouse after work hours. The only domestic work he didn't do was cook. He ate with the Hatayamas.

When I'd sit and talk with him he'd talk about his family and his week-end visits.

"My youngest boy is now out of high school," he would tell me. "He's a smart boy but I can't send him to college."

"That's too bad for him," I would say. "But you're sending Tom to Cal. That's plenty."

"Yes," he would proudly say. "I hope he'll amount to something."

Nakagawa-san's only daughter worked as a domestic in an American home and helped with the upkeep of her parents' home. Often he would tell me of his children and his eyes would shine with a far-away look.

"Why don't you stay with the family all the time, Nakagawa-san?" I'd ask him. "Why can't you get a job in Oakland and live with your family?"

He would smile. "Ah, I wish I could," he'd say. "But what could an old nursery worker do in a city? I'm too old to find other jobs. No, I must remain here."

"It's a shame," I'd tell him.

"I guess we can't have everything," he'd say and smile. "I'm lucky to have this job so long."

Several weeks after the young man had asked about Hatayama Nursery he came to see me one night. He said his name was George Murai. "I get very lonely here," he explained to me. "I never knew a nursery could be so lonely."

"You're from the city, aren't you?" I asked.

"Oakland," he said.

He was a pleasant fellow. He talked a lot and was eager. "Whenever I have the time I'm going to drop in and see you. That's if you don't mind," he said. "Over at Hatayama's I don't see any young people. I'll go crazy if I don't see somebody. In Oakland I have lots of friends."

I brought out beer and shredded shrimp. George could take beer.

"How do you like the work?" I asked him.

"Fine," he said. "I like it. Someday I'd like to have

a nursery of my own. Only I hope I get over being lonely."

"You'll be all right after you get used to it," I said.

"If I don't give up at the start I'll be all right," George said. "I don't think I'll quit. I have a girl, you see."

He pulled out of his wallet a candid shot of a young girl. "That's Lorraine Sakoda of Berkeley," he said. "Do you know her?"

I shook my head.

"We're crazy about each other," George said. "As soon as I find a steady job we're going to get married."

Before the evening was over I knew George pretty well. Several times when we mentioned friends we found them mutual. That made us feel pretty good.

After the first visit George Murai came often. He would tell me how the work progressed at Hatayama Nursery. It was getting busy. The carnation boxes had to be laid out evenly on the tracks. The soil had to be worked and shoveled in. The little carnation plants must be transplanted from the ground to the boxes. It was interesting to George.

"I'm learning everything, Takeo," he said. "Some day I'll get a nursery for myself and Lorraine."

When I went over to Hatayamas to see the boss as well as Nakagawa-san and George Murai, I would catch a glimpse of a new liveliness on the place. The eagerness of George Murai was something of a charm to watch. He would trot from one work to another as if he were eagerly playing a game. His shouts and laughter filled the nursery and the two men whose

capering days were over would look at each other and
smile. George's singing ability pleased Hatayama-san.
After supper he'd ask George to sing. George knew
only the modern popular songs.

Sometimes Nakagawa-san, George and I got together in the little house. Nakagawa-san shared the
place with George. At such times George would ask
question after question about carnation growing. He
would ask how to get rid of red spiders; how such
things as rust and spots, the menaces of the plants,
could be controlled. He would press for an answer on
how to take the crops at a specific period, how to avoid
stem rot and root rot, what fertilizers to mix, how to
take care of the cuttings. I would sit aside and listen
to Nakagawa-san answer each problem patiently and
thoroughly.

Sometimes the talk swung to Oakland. The three
of us were attached to Oakland one way or another.

"I know your son Tom pretty well," George Murai
told Nakagawa-san one night.

"Do you? Do you know Tom?" Nakagawa-san
asked eagerly.

"Sure. Tom and I used to go to Tech High together," George said. "He's going to college now."

"Sure! Sure!" Nakagawa-san said.

"I know your daughter Haruyo," George said.
"But I don't know Tetsuo so well."

Nakagawa-san nodded his head vigorously. "He's
a smart boy but I can't send him to college like Tom."

It wasn't until I was alone with Hatayama-san one
day that I began to see a change on the place. In the

latter part of August Hatayama-san was usually busy hunting around for two husky men to work on the boxes. It was the time when the old plants in the greenhouses were rooted out and the boxes filled with the old soil hauled away. Then the boxes with the new carnation plants were to be hauled in. It was the beginning of heavy work in a nursery.

This year Hatayama-san said, "I can't afford to hire more men. Flower business has been bad. We'll have no flowers to sell until November. That's a long way off. After the new boxes are in I'll have to lay off Murai boy."

"Who's going to work the boxes this year?" I asked.

"Murai and Nakagawa," Hatayama-san said. "They'll have to do it."

When the heavy work at Hatayama Nursery actually started George Murai stopped coming to see me. One afternoon when I got off early and went over there they were still out on the field. It was then I saw the struggle that knew no friendship, the deep stamp of self-preservation in human nature. Here was no flowery gesture; here were no words.

I stood and watched Nakagawa-san and George Murai push the truckloads of carnation boxes one after another without resting. In the late afternoon their sweat dried and the cool wind made the going easier. It was obvious that George being young and strong could hold a stiff pace; and that he was aware that he would be laid off when the heavy work was finished. With the last opportunity to impress the boss George did his stuff.

I was certain that Nakagawa-san sensed the young man's purpose. He stuck grimly to the pace. All this was old stuff to him. He had been through it many times. Two men were needed to lift the boxes with the old soil and toss it deftly onto the pile so that no clump of dirt would be left sticking to the boxes. Two men were needed to carefully lift the boxes with the new plants and haul them into the greenhouses. The pace which one of the men worked up could show up the weaker and the slower partner. A man could break another man with a burst of speed maintained for several days. One would be certain to break down first. When a young man set up a fast pace and held it day after day it was something for a middle-aged man to think about.

Nakagawa-san straightened as if his back ached, but he was trying to conceal it. His forearms must have been shot with needle-like pains but he worked silently.

As I watched Nakagawa-san and George Murai heaving and pushing with all their might I lost sight of the fact that they were the friends I knew. They were like strangers on a lonely road coming face to face with fear. They looked like men with no personal lives; no interests in family life, in Oakland, in Lorraine Sakoda, in the art of plant-growing, in friendship. But there it was in front of my eyes.

I turned back and went home. I wondered how they could share the little shack after what was happening on the field.

I went over several times but each night they were

so worn out with the strain of their pace they slept early. I saw them less and less. Their house was often dark and I knew they were asleep. I would then go over to see Hatayama-san.

"Come in, come in," he would greet me.

By the manner in which he talked about Nakagawa-san and George it was plain that he too had seen the struggle on the field. He would tell me how strong and fast George was. At the rate they were going they would be finished a week ahead of the last year's schedule.

"Nakagawa is getting old," he would tell me of his friend. "He's getting too old for a worker."

"He's experienced," I would reply.

"Yes," he'd say, "but George is learning fast. Already he knows very much. He's been reading about the modern method of plant growing. I've already put in an electric hotbed through George's suggestion."

Then I knew George Murai was not so close to being fired. "Are you going to keep both of them this winter?" I asked.

Hatayama-san shook his head. "No. Can't afford it. I've got to let one of them go."

Several nights later I saw lights in their little shack and went over. George was up. He was at the sink filling the kettle with water. Nakagawa-san was in bed.

"What's happened, George?" I said. "Is Nakagawa-san sick?"

"No," George said. "He's just tired. His back

aches so I'm warming it with hot water and mustard."

"I'll be all right tomorrow," Nakagawa-san said.

"You're working too hard these days, Nakagawa-san," I said. "You're straining yourself."

Nakagawa-san and George were silent. They looked at me as if I had accused them in one way or another.

Soon Nakagawa-san was back on the field. However, when I went to see how he was getting along I saw Hatayama-san out on the field with George. By the time I reached them they had pushed the truckloads of carnation boxes in and out of the greenhouses several times. George whistled when he saw me. Hatayama-san nodded his head and grinned. Something had happened to Nakagawa-san.

"I knew it was going to happen," Hatayama-san told me. "Nakagawa's getting too old for nursery work. His back troubles him again."

In the morning Nakagawa-san had stuck grimly to the work. At noon when he sat down for lunch he couldn't get up afterwards. He had to be carried to the little shack. Mrs. Hatayama applied a new plaster to his back.

"I've been on the job for two days. We'll finish on time," Hatayama-san said. "George's been a big help to me."

George looked at me and grinned.

When the pair resumed carting the boxes I went to see Nakagawa-san. As I entered the room he opened his eyes and smiled at me. He looked very tired. His repeated attempts to smile reminded me of his family and his pride for his sons.

"I'll be all right in a few days," he said eagerly. "When my back's healed I'll be like new again.

"Sure," I said. "You'll be all right."

He read to me a letter from his wife. It was filled with domestic details and his boys' activities at school. They wanted to see him soon. They missed him over the week end. They reasoned it was due to the work at the place. They missed the money too. They wanted him to be sure and bring the money for the house rent and the gas bill.

When I came away in the late afternoon Hatayama-san and George were washing their faces and hands back of the woodshed.

"How's he getting along?" Hatayama-san asked me.

"He says he's all right," I said.

"I'll go and see if he wants anything before I eat," George said.

George trotted off to the little shack. Hatayama-san motioned me toward the house. "At the end of this month I'm going to drop Nakagawa. I hate to to see him go but I must do it," he said. "Nursery is too much for him now. I hate to see him go."

"Are you really going to let him go?" I asked.

"I'm serious. He goes." He took my arm and we went inside the house. I stayed for dinner. During the courses George talked. "Someday I want to bring my girl here and introduce her," he told Hatayama-san and me. "You'll both like her."

Hatayama-san chuckled. "When will you get married, my boy?"

George smiled. "I think I can get married right away," he said.

Afterwards we listened to a few Japanese records. George got out Guy Lombardo's records and we listened to them. Mrs. Hatayama brought hot tea and Japanese teacakes. When I left George accompanied me to the road. He was in a merry mood. He whistled "I Can't Give You Anything But Love."

We said, "So long."

"Be sure to come again," he said. As I walked down the road I heard his whistling for quite a distance. When the whistling stopped the chants of the crickets in the fields became loud. Across the lot from the greenhouses I saw the little shack lit by a single light, and I knew that Nakagawa-san was not yet asleep.

Nodas In America

"HELLO, DOCTOR," I SAID, WALKING DOWN SEVENTH.

"Good morning," he answered from the other side of the street. "Nice day, isn't it?"

"Wonderful," I agreed.

I stopped and watched him go up the street. He disappeared into the doorway between two stores. He had an office upstairs. Doctor Noda. Doctor Mamoru Noda, I said to myself; and repeating the name I remembered Papa Noda.

Seven years ago I used to talk a lot with Papa Noda. I used to go over and see George, the oldest son. Papa Noda was always in the living room reading the paper. He had a twinkle in his eyes when talking to the younger generation.

"You boys are the luckiest people in the world," he used to say. "The luckiest of all."

"Why?" I used to ask.

He would smile, look around, and say nothing.

"Papa, what are you talking about?" George would scold when his father refused to answer.

The father would return to his paper for the evening, but his smile never left his face.

Time after time I would go over and see George, and Papa Noda would be sitting in the living room. Why? I would wonder. Why should he remain in the living room where the young people gathered and made rackets? Why couldn't he go in the dining room and read? During the evening I would watch him from the corner. Sometimes he would peep over his paper and watch the boys wrestling around. He never scolded us. When his daughters came in the room he would drop his paper. He would watch their little hands deftly rearrange the room and smile.

"Papa, do you want anything?" one of them would ask.

"No. Nothing," he would answer.

The girls would leave the room and the boys would continue with their roughhouse. Papa Noda's eyes would roam about the room. First, they would rest on his paintings. Then they would travel to the family portrait, his desk, and his smoking set. He would close his eyes, smile, and ease back in his sofa.

Late in the night Mama Noda would poke her head in. "Papa, tomorrow is Friday. You must get up early."

"All right, Mama," he would reply, waving his hand. "In a minute."

Papa Noda was a good storyteller. The children used to gather around him and listen. Often Mama Noda joined us. Sometimes Papa Noda's friends came and stayed.

"What would you children like to hear tonight?" Papa Noda often asked us.

"Anything, Papa," George eagerly answered.

"Anything?" Papa Noda said and smiled.

Then the seven children began to choose their favorites. George, Mamoru, Yuri, Willie, Mary Ann, Yoshio, and Betty. Papa Noda held up his hand and laughed. "I'll do the choosing," he said.

"But first, Papa, tell me," Betty said. "Why did you come to America?"

His eyes brightened. He sucked his pipe. "I came to America to seek fame and fortune. I have found my fortune."

"What is your fortune?" I asked curiously.

"Here," he said, and patted several heads of his children.

The children looked at me embarrassedly and laughed.

"Seven children," Papa Noda said proudly, counting with his fingers. "Seven treasures. I am not famous. I work all day and I am poor. But I have seven plants. Seven healthy, growing plants. Maybe one a Noguchi. Who knows?"

"Who is Noguchi?" asked Yoshio.

"Don't you know, Yoshio?" Papa Noda said incredulously.

"No. Who is he?" Yoshio asked again.

Papa Noda scratched his head. "Do you know Lincoln?"

"Sure, we know Lincoln," several voices promptly cried.

"Lincoln or Noguchi—one man. The real man, I hope to grow in my family," he said eagerly.

"Papa, tell us about your old days," Yuri cried.

"All right," Papa said, chuckling. "Did I ever tell you about my experience with eggs?"

"We heard that one but tell it again," Mamoru said.

Papa Noda settled back in the sofa and lit his pipe. The children smiled at each other and edged closer.

"Tell it from the beginning, Pop," said George.

"All right," he said, looking at the group. "I was a young boy about Yoshio's age when I came over. You should have seen Oakland at the time. Not a single store on Broadway at Fifteenth Street. Your beautiful Lake Merritt was a dirty creek. The men used to go hunting there."

"Really?" Willie said. "You didn't tell us that before."

Papa Noda smiled. "There are many stories untold. Some are lost. Others will come up in the future."

George laughed. "Broadway at Fifteenth. Just imagine! It's unbelievable."

"Your mother was still in Japan," Papa Noda said. "When I got off the boat in San Francisco I did not know which way to turn. Luckily I made acquaintances on the boat. They took me in, and we traveled all over California. None of us spoke English. We banded together in fear and bewilderment. We were adults but helpless. We just worked."

"Go on," urged Mary Ann.

"Do you know what we used to do with our money?" Papa Noda asked.

We shook our heads.

"Well, on paydays we used to deposit our money with the Japanese merchandise stores. They used to take care of our money. Banks were out of the question for us. I lost several hundred dollars that way."

"How?" Betty asked curiously.

Papa Noda smiled. "The stores would forget to pay us. We didn't think of receipts in those days."

"A bunch of suckers," George said, shaking his head.

"What did you do when Mama came to America?" Yoshio asked impatiently.

Papa Noda's eyes looked far away. "We settled in Oakland," he said. "It was our first home. I cannot forget those days. We lived in a bare house for a long time. No beds, no tables, and no chairs. We slept on floors. We collected boxes of all kinds from the stores. They came in handy. The big boxes were turned into tables. The small ones became chairs, and we stored clothes and kitchenware in others."

He paused and looked around the room. His eyes rested on the family radio and smiled.

"What about the egg incident, Papa?" Mamoru said, laughing. "Tell us that one."

Papa Noda got off the sofa and stood before us. "Remember, I cannot speak a word of English. I go into the grocer's and look around. I do not see what I wish to buy. I stand around and look all over the place. The grocer begins to talk in a strange tongue. I want eggs, I wanted to tell him. I want eggs—hen eggs. But no words."

Yoshio began to laugh loudly.

"Keep quiet, Yoshio," Yuri said.

"This is how I used to buy eggs," Papa Noda said.

He bent his body like a hen and began to peck the floor. Then he sat down like a laying hen. "Caw—ke—caw—caw—caw Caw—ke—caw—caw—caw," he cried, holding an imaginary egg.

We laughed, holding our bellies. Our laughter usually brought Mama Noda to the scene.

"Papa," Mama Noda said, smiling. "It's way past your bedtime."

"All right, Mama. I'm coming," he said, and to us whispered, "I got the eggs."

Sometimes on the way to work I would see Papa Noda at work. He would be cutting the lawn or trimming a hedge.

"Hello, young man," he would greet me. "Going to store today?"

"Yes, Papa Noda," I would reply.

"Come back here at noon and we'll have lunch together," he would say. "I have a swell banana cake I don't want."

"Thanks, but I don't want to eat up your lunch," I would tell him.

"You come back at noon. I'll be waiting for you," he would order me.

I would go back at noon and sit on the porch and share his lunch.

"Why don't you retire?" I would ask, between bites. "You have big boys. You can retire now."

"I am always a gardener. I like work," he would say proudly. "I have seven strong plants in my family, yes. They'll root in the rich California soil and grow big. Maybe some day a fine blossom."

One day in spring Papa Noda died.

After the funeral Mama Noda began to go out and find housework. For awhile the house wasn't the same. Everybody was out doing something, and I rarely went over. George became a truck driver and

brought home additional money. Mamoru found gar-
den work, but one day at the family table announced,
"I'm going to college and study medicine." Yuri and
Mary Ann got jobs in San Francisco art goods store.
George and Yuri helped Willie enter Stanford. Yoshio
and Betty were still in high school.

Several summers later George got married and I
went over to celebrate. In the living room I noticed
Papa Noda's portrait above his desk.

"That's a good picture of him," I said to Mamoru.

"It is," Mamoru said, smiling. "I wish Papa was
here tonight."

Meeting Mamoru again on the street I wanted to
see the Nodas once more: George, Yuri, Willie, Mary
Ann, Yoshio, Betty, and Mama Noda. All day I had
been thinking of the days when Papa Noda used to sit
and smile in the living room. Late in the day I hurried
over to the house, and I was met by Mama Noda at
the door.

"Oh! How good of you," she cried excitedly. "You
have come at last! Come in, come in!"

"The place hasn't changed at all," I said, looking
around. "Just like the old days."

She smiled. A baby girl toddled over to her side.

"This is Annabelle," Mama Noda said, holding up
the baby. "George's baby. She's *sansei,* you know."

"Third generation," I agreed.

"Pretty soon fourth generation," she said, smiling.

"*Shisei,*" I said, nodding my head; and we went into
the living room.

The Eggs of the World

ALMOST EVERYONE IN THE COMMUNITY KNEW SESSUE
Matoi as the heavy drinker. There was seldom a time
when one did not see him staggering full of drink.
The trouble was that the people did not know when
he was sober or drunk. He was very clever when he
was drunk and also very clever when sober. The people were afraid to touch him. They were afraid of
this man, sober or drunk, for his tongue and brains.
They dared not coax him too solicitously or make him
look ridiculous as they would treat the usual tipsy
gentleman. The people may have had only contempt
for him but they were afraid and silent. And Sessue
Matoi did little work. We always said he practically
lived on sake and wit. And that was not far from
truth.

I was at Mr. Hasegawa's when Sessue Matoi staggered in the house with several drinks under his belt.
About the only logical reason I could think of for his
visit that night was that Sessue Matoi must have
known that Mr. Hasegawa carried many bottles of
Japan-imported sake. There was no other business
why he should pay a visit to Hasegawa's. I knew Mr.
Hasegawa did not tolerate drinking bouts. He disliked
riotous scenes and people.

At first I thought Mr. Hasegawa might have been
afraid of this drinker, and Sessue Matoi had taken ad-
vantage of it. But this was not the case. Mr. Hase-

gawa was not afraid of Sessue Matoi. As I sat between the two that night I knew I was in the fun, and as likely as any minute something would explode.

"I came to see you on a very important matter, Hasegawa," Sessue Matoi said without batting an eye. "You are in a very dangerous position. You will lose your life."

"What are you talking about?" Mr. Hasegawa said.

"You are in an egg," Sessue Matoi said. "You have seen nothing but the inside of an egg and I feel sorry for you. I pity you."

"What are you talking about? Are you crazy?" Mr. Hasegawa said.

"I am not crazy. I see you very clearly in an egg," Sessue Matoi said. "That is very bad. Pretty soon you will be rotten."

Mr. Hasegawa was a serious fellow, not taking to laughter and gaiety. But he laughed out loud. This was ridiculous. Then he remembered Sessue Matoi was drunk.

"What about this young fellow?" Mr. Hasegawa said, pointing at me.

Sessue Matoi looked me over quizzically. He appeared to study me from all angles. Then he said, "His egg is forming. Pretty soon he must break the shell of his egg or little later will find himself too weak to do anything about it."

I said nothing. Mr. Hasegawa sat with a twinkle in his eyes.

"What about yourself, Sessue Matoi?" he said. "Do you live in an egg?"

"No," Sessue Matoi said. "An egg is when you are walled in, a prisoner within yourself. I am free, I have broken the egg long ago. You see as I am. I am not hidden beneath a shell and I am not enclosed in one either. I am walking on this earth with my good feet, and also I am drinking and enjoying, but am sad on seeing so many eggs in the world, unbroken, untasted, and rotten."

"Are you insulting the whole world or are you just insulting me?" Mr. Hasegawa said.

"I am insulting no one. Look, look me in the eye, Hasgawa. See how sober I am," he said. "I am not insulting you. I love you. I love the whole world and sober or drunk it doesn't make a bit of difference. But when I say an egg's an egg I mean it. You can't very well break the eggs I see."

"Couldn't you break the eggs for us?" Mr. Hasegawa said. "You seem to see the eggs very well. Couldn't you go around and break the shells and make this world the hatching ground?"

"No, no!" Sessue Matoi said. "You have me wrong! I cannot break the eggs. You cannot break the eggs. You can break an egg though."

"I don't get you," said Mr. Hasegawa.

"An egg is broken from within," said Sessue Matoi. "The shell of an egg melts by itself through heat or warmth and it's natural, and independent."

"This is ridiculous," said Mr. Hasegawa. "An egg can be broken from outside. You know very well an egg may be broken by a rap from outside."

"You can rape and assault too," said Sessue Matoi.

"This is getting to be fantastic," Mr. Hasegawa said. "This is silly! Here we are getting all burned up over a little egg, arguing over nonsense."

"This is very important to me," Sessue Matoi said. "Probably the only thing I know about. I study egg culture twenty-four hours. I live for it."

"And for sake," Mr. Hasegawa said.

"And for sake," Sessue Matoi said.

"Shall we study about sake tonight? Shall we taste the sake and you tell me about the flavor?" Mr Hasegawa said.

"Fine, fine, fine!" said Mr. Matoi.

Mr. Hasegawa went back in the kitchen and we heard him moving about. Pretty soon he came back with a steaming bottle of sake. "This is Hakushika," he said.

"Fine, fine," Sessue Matoi said. "All brands are the same to me, all flavors match my flavor. When I drink I am drinking my flavor."

Mr. Hasegawa poured him several cups which Sessue Matoi promptly gulped down. Sessue Matoi gulped down several more. "Ah, when I drink sake I think of the eggs in the world," he said. "All the unopened eggs in the world."

"Just what are you going to do with all these eggs lying about? Aren't you going to do something about it? Can't you put some of the eggs aside and heat them up or warm them and help break the shells from within?" Mr. Hasegawa said.

"No," Sessue Matoi said. "I am doing nothing of the sort. If I do all you think I should do, then I will have no time to sit and drink. And I must drink. I cannot go a day without drinking because when I drink I am really going outward, not exactly drinking but expressing myself outwardly, talking very much and saying little, sadly and pathetically."

"Tell me, Sessue Matoi," said Mr. Hasegawa. "Are you sad at this moment? Aren't you happy in your paganistic fashion, drinking and laughing through twenty-four hours?"

"Now, you are feeling sorry for me, Hasegawa," Sessue Matoi said. "You are getting sentimental. Don't think of me in that manner. Think of me as the mess I am. I am a mess. Then laugh very hard, keep laughing very hard. Say, oh what an egg he has opened up! Look at the shells, look at the drunk without a bottle."

"Why do you say these things?" Mr. Hasegawa said. "You are very bitter."

"I am not bitter, I am not mad at anyone," Sessue Matoi said. "But you are still talking through the eggshell."

"You are insulting me again," Mr. Hasegawa said. "Do not allow an egg to come between us."

"That is very absurd," Sessue Matoi said, rising from his chair. "You are very absurd, sir. An egg is the most important and the most disturbing thing in the world. Since you are an egg you do not know an egg. That is sad. I say, good night, gentlemen."

Sessue Matoi in all seriousness bowed formally and then tottered to the door.

"Wait, Sessue Matoi," said Mr. Hasegawa. "You

didn't tell me what you thought of the flavor of my sake."

"I did tell you," Sessue Matoi said. "I told you the flavor right along."

"That's the first time I ever heard you talking about the flavor of sake tonight," said Mr. Hasegawa.

"You misunderstand me again," said Sessue Matoi. "When you wish to taste the flavor of sake which I drank then you must drink the flavor which I have been spouting all evening. Again, good night, gentlemen."

Again he bowed formally at the door and staggered out of the house.

I was expecting to see Mr. Hasegawa burst out laughing the minute Sessue Matoi stepped out of the house. He didn't. "I suppose he will be around in several days to taste your sake. This must happen every time he comes to see you," I said.

"No," Mr. Hasegawa said. "Strangely, this is the first time he ever walked out like that. I cannot understand him. I don't believe he will be back for a long time."

"Was he drunk or sober tonight?" I said.

"I really don't know," said Mr. Hasegawa. "He must be sober and drunk at the same time."

"Do you really think we will not see him for awhile?" I said.

"Yes, I am very sure of it. To think that an egg would come between us!"

He Who Has the Laughing Face

THE SIMPLEST THING TO SAY OF HIM IS THAT HE IS sad and alone but is laughing all the time. It would definitely put him in a hole and everybody would understand and say what a sad story, what an unhappy man he is, what bravery there is in the world. But that is not the story. He is a very common man. His kind is almost everywhere, his lot is the ordinary, the most common, and that is why he is so lost and hidden away from the spotlight.

He, the Japanese, was sitting on the park bench on Seventh and Harrison, looking and gazing at the people without much thought but looking just the same and this being Sunday he was taking his time about it, taking all the time in the world, to belong to this great world or to discover why he is so unhappy, sad and alone. But he did not think for long, he did not sit down and probe like great philosophers do. Instead he simply sat and pretty soon from his sadness, and aloneness, he began to smile, not from happiness, not from sadness, and this is where I saw his face, not a handsome one but common and of everyday life.

His name does not matter, it makes no difference, although it is Tsumura. I found him sitting on the park bench on Seventh and Harrison when I looked up from a book I was reading under a tree. And before one begins to guess and attempt to judge a person right who is a stranger, there is an adventure. I sat, pretending to read the book, and all the time watching this individual who was like all or any of the park bench sitters on Sundays. By the time I began to guess who he was and what he did, he was someone of immense proportions, someone living close to me or someone I know and talk to. And then suddenly, unexpectedly, he would laugh. Not a crazy laugh. He would laugh the kind no one pays attention to. Or if someone pays attention and hear him that someone will believe the man had seen something funny in the park or in the street or had listened to something amusing, and let it go. But that is not all. He did not look queer, he looked the part of others—out for rest.

When I began to guess who he was and what he did there was no stopping of human curiosity and there was no end of mental adventure that is inward and centralized on intuition. What was he laughing at? I wanted to know. Who was he, what does he do for a living? I sat and guessed many times.

He looked like a writer or an artist or a composer with his sad face detached from laughter. But he was laughing almost all the time and smiling as if the world was a part of him. He looked like an idiot, laughing when there was no outward evidence of laughing matter and sense. But idiot he could not be—he was too polished, too well groomed to lead a causeless life. Could he be a priest, a clergy? Could he be the one to lead others and could he by chance come among the people to mix without indentity, without the strings attached to him? But on Sunday! Sunday is the clergyman's busy day and also, Sunday is the day anyone may possibly be in the park. At one time I believed he was a grocer or a manager of a dry goods store or the proprietor of a flower shop. So it went but it did not end.

One Monday morning I saw him out early in the park, sitting and looking the same as he did the day before and on other Sundays, watching the race of people and of machinery and of time passing through the earth with the same lazy, easy eyes of Sunday and looking unhurried and unflustered and still living, in spite of the fact that this was the restless weekday, the day of sweat and toil and misery and no church bells ringing. He sat without words, like other days, simply sitting and laughing at intervals unconsciously, unaware of human ears and human eyes listening and noticing and probing him. He sat without austerity, without a wit of sadness, sitting, basking, drinking, not singing dramatically in the opera or in the arena, not writing to bring tears or happiness, not using, not playing, not living heroically in one word perhaps, but alive, basking today, a living presence, a phenomenon of life that is here awhile and gone without an answer.

And then on Tuesday I saw him again, and again on Wednesday, Thursday, Friday till I began to believe I have been following a man of leisure or a man out of work or on pension. This assumption, however, was short lived. He did not make an appearance for a week, leaving myself sitting under a tree, waiting with anticipation and with nervousness that the man will not appear again. When I sat and watched for a week and he did not come, I was certain I had lost him, the

individual who had become someone big, the man who
instantly had charged the park on Seventh and Harrison with life and interest. I sat and read my book
regretting the opportunity I had lost to identify him,
to put him down as he was, to seek him out through
words and gestures the man he really was in the material atmosphere.

But the Japanese returned to the park bench one
Sunday, returning with laughter intact and with the
sadness creased in his face, looking unchanged as the
time I had first noticed him, looking and laughing at
intervals, unexpectedly and inconspicuously, occupying a place on the park bench, occupying simply and
quietly and lost in the mass of Sunday faces.

This time I did not hesitate to go up to the park
bench and address him. I said hello and he looked at
me not surprised and smiled. I told him I had been
sitting under the tree reading books for weeks and that
I had seen him come and sit down on the park bench
for weeks and that for a week I had missed him and
feared that something must have happened or more
dreadful, that he was not to appear at the park bench
again.

"Sit down," he said.

He made room for me. We sat and talked a good
hour or more. He said his name was Tsumura, and he
was from Shinano prefecture in Japan. I said my
parents were from Hiroshima prefecture and he said
he knew a number of people from Hiroshima.

"I was afraid I had lost you, that I would not see
you again," I said.

The man laughed. "You need not be afraid," he said. "I am always here. I am not rich and I do not travel.

"What do you do?" I said.

He said he worked for Hinode Laundry Co. He said he was a truck driver calling at the houses and offices all over the East Bay. He said he had been working for fourteen years at the same place and sometimes he worked only part time which was why I saw him on weekdays for a long stretch.

A moment later he said he had to go. He said the supper at the laundry house was at six and he must go now to be on time. We said good-bye and promised that we would meet again. Not a word did he say about the sadness of his face and his life. And I did not ask why he is sad and why he is laughing all the time. We did not speak a word of it, we did not like to be foolish and ask and answer the problem of the earth, and we did not have to. Every little observation, every little banal talk or laughing matter springs from the sadness of the earth that is reality; every meeting between individuals, every meeting of society, every meeting of a gathering, of gaiety or sorrow, springs from sadness that is the bed of earth and truth.

And so when he said he was a laundry truck driver and had come to the park for breath of air which is no different from the wind that hits him while driving, all that matters is that he is a laundry truck driver, a man living in the city, coming to the park for a pause, not for great thoughts or to escape the living of life, but to pause and laugh, unbitterly and unsentimentally, not wishing for dreams, not expecting a miracle, not even accepting the turn of the next hour or the next second.

And this is the greatest thing happening today: that of a laundry truck driver or an equivalent to such who is living and coming in and out of parks, the homes, the alleys, the dives, the offices, the rendezvous, the vices, the churches, the operas, the movies; all seeking unconsciously, unawaredly, the hold of this sadness, the loneliness, the barrenness, which is not elusive but hovering and pervading and seeping into the flesh and vegetation alike, churning out potentially the greatness, the weakness, and the heroism, the cowardice; and therefore, leaving unfinished all the causes of sadness, unhappiness, and sorrows of the earth behind in the laughter and the mute silence of time.

Slant-Eyed Americans

MY MOTHER WAS COMMENTING ON THE FINE CALI-
fornia weather. It was Sunday noon, December 7.
We were having our lunch, and I had the radio going.
"Let's take the afternoon off and go to the city," I
said to Mother.

"All right. We shall go," she said dreamily. "Ah,
four months ago my boy left Hayward to join the
army, and a fine send-off he had. Our good friends—
ah, I shall never forget the day of his departure."

"We'll visit some of our friends in Oakland and
then take in a movie," I said. "Care to come along,
Papa?"

Father shook his head. "No, I'll stay home and take
it easy."

"That's his heaven," Mother commented. "To stay
home, read the papers over and over, and smoke his
Bull Durham."

I laughed. Suddenly the musical program was cut
off as a special announcement came over the air: At
7:25 a.m. this morning a squadron of Japanese bomb-
ing planes attacked Pearl Harbor. The battle is still
in progress.

"What's this? Listen to the announcement," I cried,
going to the radio.

Abruptly the announcement stopped and the musi-
cale continued.

"What is it?" Mother asked. "What has happened?"

"The radio reports that the Japanese planes attacked Hawaii this morning," I said incredulously. "It couldn't be true."

"It must be a mistake. Couldn't it have been a part of a play?" asked Mother.

I dialed other stations. Several minutes later one of the stations confirmed the bulletin.

"It must be true," Father said quietly.

I said, "Japan has declared war on the United States and Great Britain."

The room became quiet but for the special bulletin coming in every now and then.

"It cannot be true, yet it must be so," Father said over and over.

"Can it be one of those programs scaring the people about invasion?" Mother asked me.

"No, I'm sure this is a news report," I replied.

Mother's last ray of hope paled and her eyes became dull. "Why did it have to happen? The common people in Japan don't want war, and we don't want war. Here the people are peace-loving. Why cannot the peoples of the earth live together peacefully?"

"Since Japan declared war on the United States it'll mean that you parents of American citizens have become enemy aliens," I said.

"Enemy aliens," my mother whispered.

Night came but sleep did not come. We sat up late in the night hoping against hope that some good news would come, retracting the news of vicious attack and open hostilities.

"This is very bad for the people with Japanese faces," I said.

Father slowly shook his head.

"What shall we do?" asked Mother.

"What can we do?" Father said helplessly.

At the flower market next morning the growers were present but the buyers were scarce. The place looked empty and deserted. "Our business is shot to pieces," one of the boys said.

"Who'll buy flowers now?" another called.

Don Haley, the seedsman, came over looking bewildered. "I suppose you don't need seeds now."

We shook our heads.

"It looks bad," I said. "Will it affect your business?"

"Flower seed sale will drop but the vegetable seeds will move quicker," Don said. "I think I'll have to put more time on the vegetable seeds."

Nobu Hiramatsu who had been thinking of building another greenhouse joined us. He had plans to grow more carnations and expand his business.

"What's going to happen to your plans, Nobu?" asked one of the boys.

"Nothing. I'm going to sit tight and see how the things turn out," he said.

"Flowers and war don't go together," Don said. "You cannot concentrate too much on beauty when destruction is going about you."

"Sure, pretty soon we'll raise vegetables instead of flowers," Grasselli said.

A moment later the market opened and we went

back to the tables to sell our flowers. Several buyers came in and purchased a little. The flowers didn't move at all. Just as I was about to leave the place I met Tom Yamashita, the Nisei gardener with a future.

"What are you doing here, Tom? What's the matter with your work?" I asked as I noticed his pale face.

"I was too sick with yesterday's news so I didn't work," he said. "This is the end. I am done for."

"No, you're not. Buck up, Tom," I cried. "You have a good future, don't lose hope."

"Sometimes I feel all right. You are an American, I tell myself. Devote your energy and life to the American way of life. Long before this my mind was made up to become a true American. This morning my Caucasian American friends sympathized with me. I felt good and was grateful. Our opportunity has come to express ourselves and act. We are Americans in thought and action. I felt like leaping to work. Then I got sick again because I got to thinking that Japan was the country that attacked the United States. I wanted to bury myself for shame."

I put my hand on his shoulder. "We all feel the same way, Tom. We're human so we flounder around awhile when an unexpected and big problem confronts us, but now that situation has to be passed by. We can't live in the same stage long. We have to move along, face the reality no matter what's in store for us."

Tom stood silently.

"Let's go to my house and take the afternoon off," I suggested. "We'll face a new world tomorrow morning with boldness and strength. What do you say, Tom?"

"All right," Tom agreed.

At home Mother was anxiously waiting for me. When she saw Tom with me her eyes brightened. Tom Yamashita was a favorite of my mother's.

"Look, a telegram from Kazuo!" she cried to me, holding up an envelope. "Read it and tell me what he says."

I tore it open and read. "He wants us to send $45 for train fare. He has a good chance for a furlough."

Mother fairly leaped in the air with the news. She had not seen my brother for four months. "How wonderful! This can happen only in America."

Suddenly she noticed Tom looking glum, and pushed him in the house. "Cheer up, Tom. This is no time for young folks to despair. Roll up your sleeves and get to work. America needs you."

Tom smiled for the first time and looked at me.

"See, Tom?" I said. "She's quick to recover. Yesterday she was wilted, and she's seventy-three."

"Tom, did you go to your gardens today?" she asked him.

"No."

"Why not?" she asked, and then added quickly. "You young men should work hard all the more, keeping up the normal routine of life. You ought to know, Tom, that if everybody dropped their work everything would go to seed. Who's going to take care of the gardens if you won't?"

Tom kept still.

Mother poured tea and brought the cookies. "Don't worry about your old folks. We have stayed here to belong to the American way of life. Time will tell our true purpose. We remained in America for permanence—not for temporary convenience. We common people need not fear."

"I guess you are right," Tom agreed.

"And America is right. She cannot fail. Her principles will stand the test of time and tyranny. Someday agression will be outlawed by all nations."

Mother left the room to prepare the dinner. Tom got up and began to walk up and down the room. Several times he looked out the window and watched the wind blow over the field.

"Yes, if the gardens are ruined I'll rebuild them," he said. "I'll take charge of every garden in the city. All the gardens of America for that matter. I'll rebuild them as fast as the enemies wreck them. We'll have nature on our side and you cannot crush nature."

I smiled and nodded. "Good for you! Tomorrow we'll get up early in the morning and work, sweat, and create. Let's shake on it."

We solemnly shook hands, and by the grip of his fingers I knew he was ready to lay down his life for America and for his gardens.

"No word from him yet," Mother said worriedly. "He should have arrived yesterday. What's happened to him?"

It was eight in the evening, and we had had no word from my brother for several days.

"He's not coming home tonight. It's too late now," I said. "He should have arrived in Oakland this morning at the latest."

Our work had piled up and we had to work late into the night. There were still some pompons to bunch. Faintly the phone rang in the house.

"The phone!" cried Mother excitedly. "It's Kazuo, sure enough."

In the flurry of several minutes I answered the phone, greeted my brother, and was on my way to San Leandro to drive him home. On the way I tried to think of the many things I wanted to say. From the moment I spotted him waiting on the corner I could not say the thing I wanted to. I took his bag and he got in the car, and for some time we did not say anything. Then I asked him how the weather had been in Texas and how he had been.

"We were waiting for you since yesterday," I said. "Mother is home getting the supper ready. You haven't eaten yet, have you?"

He shook his head. "The train was late getting into Los Angeles. We were eight hours behind time and I should have reached San Francisco this morning around eight."

Reaching home it was the same way. Mother could not say anything. "We have nothing special tonight, wish we had something good."

"Anything would do, Mama," my brother said.

Father sat in the room reading the papers but his eyes were over the sheet and his hands were trembling. Mother scurried about getting his supper ready. I sat across the table from my brother, and in the silence which was action I watched the wave of emotions in the room. My brother was aware of it too. He sat there without a word, but I knew he understood. Not many years ago he was the baby of the family, having never been away from home. Now he was on his own, his quiet confidence actually making him appear larger. Keep up the fire, that was his company's motto. It was evident that he was a soldier. He had gone beyond life and death matter, where the true soldiers of war or peace must travel, and had returned.

For five short days we went about our daily task, picking and bunching the flowers for Christmas, eating heavy meals, and visiting the intimates. It was as if we were waiting for the hour of his departure, the time being so short. Every minute was crowded with privacy, friends, and nursery work. Too soon the time for his train came but the family had little to talk.

"Kazuo, don't worry about home or me," Mother said as we rode into town.

"Take care of yourself," my brother told her.

At the 16th Street Station Mother's close friend was waiting for us. She came to bid my brother goodbye. We had fifteen minutes to wait. My brother bought a copy of *The Coast* to see if his cartoons were in.

"Are you in this month's issue?" I asked.

"I haven't seen it yet," he said, leafing the pages. "Yes, I'm in. Here it is."

"Good!" I said. "Keep trying hard. Someday peace

will come, and when you return laughter will reign once again."

My mother showed his cartoon to her friend. The train came in and we got up. It was a long one. We rushed to the Los Angeles-bound coach.

Mother's friend shook hands with my brother. "Give your best to America. Our people's honor depend on you Nisei soldiers."

My brother nodded and then glanced at Mother. For a moment her eyes twinkled and she nodded. He waved good-bye from the platform. Once inside the train we lost him. When the train began to move my mother cried, "Why doesn't he pull up the shades and look out? Others are doing it."

We stood and watched until the last of the train was lost in the night of darkness.

The Trees

"GOOD MORNING, HASHIMOTO, GOOD MORNING," FU-kushima said to his friend.

"Ah, Fukushima, what do you want?" Hashimoto said.

Fukushima rubbed his hands and stomped his feet. "It is cold. The sun is not warm enough."

Hashimoto laughed. "You are usually asleep at this time," he said. "What do you want at this early hour?"

"I came to see you and the pine trees," Fukushima said. "Do you not walk among your trees every morning?"

"Yes, you know that," said Hashimoto.

"Did you already take a walk this morning? I want to walk with you among your pine trees," said Fukushima.

"No, not yet," Hashimoto said, looking curiously. "I am going to my garden now. Come on, friend."

The two walked to the rear of the house. The sun climbed higher and the garden became warm. They walked among the pine trees. They crossed many times the little stream running alongside the path. The sparrows chattered noisily overhead. The two circled the garden several times. Then they went up and down many times, crisscrossed, and finally sat down to rest on an old stone bench.

"Hashimoto, I am your old-time friend," Fukushima said. "What do you see in the trees?"

Hashimoto looked sharply at his friend. "Why, I see the trees," he said a moment later.

"No, I do not mean it that way," Fukushima said. "That is a common expression. I want you to tell me how you really see these pine trees."

Hashimoto laughed.

"Please. I am your friend," Fukushima said. "Please tell me your secret of happiness."

"Fukushima, there is really nothing in it. I simply see the trees. That is all."

"No, that is not all. Why, anyone could see the trees," Fukushima said.

"They could and should," Hashimoto agreed.

"I came here early to see the trees. I have walked with you among the trees, and still I don't see anything in the trees. Why is that?" asked Fukushima.

The two friends looked silently at each other.

"Did you not say you were cold a few minutes ago?" Hashimoto said.

"Yes, I was cold," Fukushima admitted.

"Look at yourself now," Hashimoto said. "You are warm and perspiring. You are very warm."

"What of it? That is a fact," said Fukushima. "What are you talking about?"

"The difference between warmth and cold is movement," said Hashimoto. "And movement makes warmth and cold."

"Hashimoto, I do not want to hear about warmth and cold," pleaded Fukushima. "I want to share your happiness. I want you to explain the trees you see."

"I cannot explain the trees, Fukushima," Hashimoto said. "But listen, friend. The warmth and cold I talk about is in the trees."

Fukushima shook his head. "You are not my friend. You do not want to tell me your secret."

Hashimoto shook his head. "You are my friend, and the secret you mention is the most exposed of all."

Fukushima looked coldly at Hashimoto. "If you do not tell me your secret we shall be friends no more. You know what happened to me. A year ago I was fairly rich. I owned stocks and properties. And then fate overtook me and I lost all. I am a defeated man but I want to fight on, and I came to you."

Hashimoto nodded. "Let us try again. You were cold when you came here, but when you walked about the garden you became warm and experienced warmth. Do you see, Fukushima? You would not have known warmth if you did not walk?"

"But the trees—people tell me you have your trees, and that is why you are happy," Fukushima said.

Hashimoto shook his head sadly. His eyes roamed about the garden.

"Why are you so happy?" asked Fukushima.

"I am not always happy," cried Hashimoto. "I am cold and warm too."

"Our age is unkind to men," Fukushima said bitterly. "And you do not help a friend."

"I have tried my best," Hashimoto said.

"Some day you will see me join our friend Makino. I will join him at the crazy hospital in Stockton. He reads many books like you but he went crazy," Fukushima said.

The two looked at each other silently.

"Hashimoto, when I leave here today I shall never see you again. Please, tell me," begged Fukushima.

Hashimoto looked up eagerly. "All right, listen. You were cold when you came here, but when you walked about. . . ."

"I do not want to hear any more!" cried Fukushima, leaping furiously to his feet. "If you cannot tell me about the trees do not talk!"

"Fukushima," cried Hashimoto. "Fukushima!"

He stood by the old stone bench and watched his friend go out the gate and into the highway.

The Six Rows of Pompons

WHEN LITTLE NEPHEW TATSUO CAME TO LIVE WITH us he liked to do everything the adults were doing on the nursery, and although his little mind did not know it, everything he did was the opposite of adult conduct, unknowingly destructive and disturbing. So Uncle Hiroshi after witnessing several weeks of rampage said, "This has got to stop, this sawing the side of a barn and nailing the doors to see if it would open. But we must not whip him. We must not crush his curiosity by any means."

And when Nephew Tatsuo, who was seven and in high second grade, got used to the place and began coming out into the fields and pestering us with difficult questions as "What are the plants here for? What is water? Why are the bugs made for? What are the birds and why do the birds sing?" and so on, I said to Uncle Hiroshi, "We must do something about this. We cannot answer questions all the time and we cannot be correct all the time and so we will do harm. But something must be done about this beyond a doubt."

"Let us take him in our hands," Uncle Hiroshi said.

So Uncle Hiroshi took little Nephew Tatsuo aside, and brought him out in the fields and showed him the many rows of pompons growing. "Do you know what these are?" Uncle Hiroshi said. "These things here?"

"Yes. Very valuable," Nephew Tatsuo said. "Plants."

"Do you know when these plants grow up and flower, we eat?" Uncle Hiroshi said.

Nephew Tatsuo nodded. "Yes," he said, "I knew that."

"All right. Uncle Hiroshi will give you six rows of pompons," Uncle Hiroshi said. "You own these six rows. You take care of them. Make them grow and flower like your uncles'."

"Gee!" Nephew Tatsuo said.

"Do you want to do it?" Uncle Hiroshi said.

"Sure!" he said.

"Then jump right in and start working," Uncle Hiroshi said. "But first, let me tell you something. You cannot quit once you start. You must not let it die, you must make it grow and flower like your uncles'."

"All right," little Nephew Tatsuo said, "I will."

"Every day you must tend to your plants. Even after the school opens, rain or shine," Uncle Hiroshi said.

"All right," Nephew Tatsuo said. "You'll see!"

So the old folks once more began to work peacefully, undisturbed, and Nephew Tatsuo began to work on his plot. However, every now and then Nephew Tatsuo would run to Uncle Hiroshi with much excitement.

"Uncle Hiroshi, come!" he said. "There's bugs on my plants! Big bugs, green bugs with black dots and some brown bugs. What shall I do?"

"They're bad bugs," Uncle Hiroshi said. "Spray them."

"I have no spray," Nephew Tatsuo said excitedly.

"All right. I will spray them for you today," Uncle Hiroshi said. "Tomorrow I will get you a small hand spray. Then you must spray your own plants."

Several tall grasses shot above the pompons and Uncle Hiroshi noticed this. Also, he saw the beds beginning to fill with young weeds.

"Those grasses attract the bugs," he said. "Take them away. Keep the place clean."

It took Nephew Tatsuo days to pick the weeds out of the six beds. And since the weeds were not picked cleanly, several weeks later it looked as if it was not touched at all. Uncle Hiroshi came around sometimes to feel the moisture in the soil. "Tatsuo," he said, "your plants need water. Give it plenty, it is summer. Soon it will be too late."

Nephew Tatsuo began watering his plants with the three-quarter hose.

"Don't hold the hose long in one place and short in another," Uncle Hiroshi said. "Keep it even and wash the leaves often."

In October Uncle Hiroshi's plants stood tall and straight and the buds began to appear. Nephew Tatsuo kept at it through summer and autumn, although at times he looked wearied and indifferent. And each time Nephew Tatsuo's enthusiasm lagged Uncle Hiroshi took him over to the six rows of pompons and appeared greatly surprised.

"Gosh," he said, "your plants are coming up! It is growing rapidly; pretty soon the flowers will come."

"Do you think so?" Nephew Tatsuo said.

"Sure, can't you see it coming?" Uncle Hiroshi said. "You will have lots of flowers. When you have enough to make a bunch I will sell it for you at the flower market."

"Really?" Nephew Tatsuo said. "In the flower market?"

Uncle Hiroshi laughed. "Sure," he said. "That's where the plant business goes on, isn't it?"

One day Nephew Tatsuo wanted an awful lot to have us play catch with him with a tennis ball. It was at the time when the nursery was the busiest and even Sundays were all work.

"Nephew Tatsuo, don't you realize we are all men with responsibilities?" Uncle Hiroshi said. "Uncle Hiroshi has lots of work to do today. Now is the busiest time. You also, have lots of work to do in your beds. And this should be your busiest time. Do you know whether your pompons are dry or wet?"

"No, Uncle Hiroshi," he said. "I don't quite remember."

"Then attend to it. Attend to it," Uncle Hiroshi said.

Nephew Tatsuo ran to the six rows of pompons to see if it was dry or wet. He came running back. "Uncle Hiroshi, it is still wet," he said.

"All right," Uncle Hiroshi said, "but did you see those holes in the ground with the piled-up mounds of earth?"

"Yes. They're gopher holes," Nephew Tatsuo said.

"Right," Uncle Hiroshi said. "Did you catch the gopher?"

"No," said Nephew Tatsuo.

"Then attend to it, attend to it right away," Uncle Hiroshi said.

One day in late October Uncle Hiroshi's pompons began to bloom. He began to cut and bunch and take them early in the morning to the flower market in Oakland. And by this time Nephew Tatsuo was anxious to see his pompons bloom. He was anxious to see how it feels to cut the flowers of his plants. And by this time Nephew Tatsuo's six beds of pompons looked like a patch of tall weeds left uncut through the summer. Very few pompon buds stood out above the tangle.

Few plants survived out of the six rows. In some parts of the beds where the pompons had plenty of water and freedom, the stems grew strong and tall and the buds were big and round. Then there were parts where the plants looked shriveled and the leaves were wilted and brown. The majority of the plants were dead before the cool weather arrived. Some died by dryness, some by gophers or moles, and some were dwarfed by the great big grasses which covered the pompons altogether.

When Uncle Hiroshi's pompons began to flower everywhere the older folks became worried.

"We must do something with Tatsuo's six beds. It is worthless and his bugs are coming over to our beds,"

Tatsuo's father said. "Let's cut it down and burn them today."

"No," said Uncle Hiroshi. "That will be a very bad thing to do. It will kill Nephew Tatsuo. Let the plants stay."

So the six beds of Nephew Tatsuo remained intact, the grasses, the gophers, the bugs, the buds and the plants and all. Soon after, the buds began to flower and Nephew Tatsuo began to run around calling Uncle Hiroshi. He said the flowers are coming. Big ones, good ones. He wanted to know when can he cut them.

"Today," Uncle Hiroshi said. "Cut it today and I will sell it for you at the market tomorrow."

Next day at the flower market Uncle Hiroshi sold the bunch of Nephew Tatsuo's pompons for twenty-five cents. When he came home Nephew Tatsuo ran to the car.

"Did you sell it, Uncle Hiroshi?" Nephew Tatsuo said.

"Sure. Why would it not sell?" Uncle Hiroshi said. "They are healthy, carefully cultured pompons."

Nephew Tatsuo ran around excitedly. First, he went to his father. "Papa!" he said, "someone bought my pompons!" Then he ran over to my side and said, "The bunch was sold! Uncle Hiroshi sold my pompons!"

At noontime, after the lunch was over, Uncle Hiroshi handed over the quarter to Nephew Tatsuo.

"What shall I do with this money?" asked Nephew Tatsuo, addressing all of us, with shining eyes.

"Put it in your toy bank," said Tatsuo's father.

"No," said Uncle Hiroshi. "Let him do what he wants. Let him spend and have a taste of his money."

"Do you want to spend your quarter, Nephew Tatsuo?" I said.

"Yes," he said.

"Then do anything you wish with it," Uncle Hiroshi said. "Buy anything you want. Go and have a good time. It is your money."

On the following Sunday we did not see Nephew Tatsuo all day. When he came back late in the afternoon Uncle Hiroshi said, "Nephew Tatsuo, what did you do today?"

"I went to a show, then I bought an ice cream cone and then on my way home I watched the baseball game at the school, and then I bought a popcorn from the candy man. I have five cents left," Nephew Tatsuo said.

"Good," Uncle Hiroshi said. "That shows a good spirit."

Uncle Hiroshi, Tatsuo's father, and I sat in the shade. It was still hot in the late afternoon that day. We sat and watched Nephew Tatsuo riding around and around the yard on his red tricycle, making a furious dust.

"Next year he will forget what he is doing this year and will become a wild animal and go on a rampage again," the father of Tatsuo said.

"Next year is not yet here," said Uncle Hiroshi.

"Do you think he will be interested to raise pompons again?" the father said.

"He enjoys praise," replied Uncle Hiroshi, "and he takes pride in good work well done. We will see."

"He is beyond a doubt the worst gardener in the country," I said. "Probably he is the worst in the world."

"Probably," said Uncle Hiroshi.

"Tomorrow he will forget how he enjoyed spending his year's income," the father of Tatsuo said.

"Let him forget," Uncle Hiroshi said. "One year is nothing. We will keep this six rows of pompon business up till he comes to his senses."

We sat that night the whole family of us, Uncle Hiroshi, Nephew Tatsuo's father, I, Nephew Tatsuo, and the rest, at the table and ate, and talked about the year and the prospect of the flower business, about Uncle Hiroshi's pompon crop, and about Nephew Tatsuo's work and, also, his unfinished work in this world.

Business at Eleven

WHEN HE CAME TO OUR HOUSE ONE DAY AND
knocked on the door and immediately sold me a copy
of *The Saturday Evening Post*, it was the beginning of
our friendship and also, the beginning of our business
relationship.

His name is John. I call him Johnny and he is eleven.
It is the age when he should be crazy about baseball or
football or fishing. But he isn't. Instead he came again
to our door and made a business proposition.

"I think you have many old magazines here," he
said.

"Yes," I said, "I have magazines of all kinds in the
basement."

"Will you let me see them?" he said.

"Sure," I said.

I took him down to the basement where the stacks
of magazines stood in the corner. Immediately this
little boy went over to the piles and lifted a number of
magazines and examined the dates of each number and
the names.

"Do you want to keep these?" he said.

"No. You can have them," I said.

"No. I don't want them for nothing," he said.
"How much do you want for them?"

"You can have them for nothing," I said.

"No, I want to buy them," he said. "How much
do you want for them?"

This was a boy of eleven, all seriousness and purpose. "What are you going to do with the old magazines?" "I am going to sell them to people," he said.

We arranged the financial matters satisfactorily. We agreed he was to pay three cents for each copy he took home. On the first day he took home an *Esquire*, a couple of old *Saturday Evening Posts*, a *Scribner's* an *Atlantic Monthly*, and a *Collier's*. He said he would be back soon to buy more magazines.

When he came back several days later, I learned his name was John so I began calling him Johnny.

"How did you make out, Johnny?" I said.

"I sold them all," he said. "I made seventy cents altogether."

"Good for you," I said. "How do you manage to get seventy cents for old magazines?"

Johnny said as he made the rounds selling the *Saturday Evening Post*, he also asked the folks if there were any back numbers they particularly wanted. Sometimes, he said, people will pay unbelievable prices for copies they had missed and wanted very much to see some particular articles or pictures, or their favorite writers' stories.

"You are a smart boy," I said.

"Papa says, if I want to be a salesman, be a good salesman," Johnny said. "I'm going to be a good salesman."

"That's the way to talk," I said. "And what does your father do?"

"Dad doesn't do anything. He stays at home," Johnny said.

"Is he sick or something?" I said.

"No, he isn't sick," he said. "He's all right. There's nothing wrong with him."

"How long have you been selling *The Saturday Evening Post?*" I asked.

"Five years," he said. "I began at six."

"Your father is lucky to have a smart boy like you for a son," I said.

That day he took home a dozen or so of the old magazines. He said he had five standing orders, an *Esquire* issue of June 1937, *Atlantic Monthly* February 1938 number, a copy of December 11, 1937 issue of *New Yorker*, *Story Magazine* of February 1934 and a *Collier's* of April 2, 1938. The others, he said, he was taking a chance at.

"I can sell them," Johnny said.

Several days later I saw Johnny again at the door.

"Hello, Johnny," I said. "Did you sell them already?"

"Not all," he said. "I have two left. But I want some more."

"All right," I said. "You must have good business."

"Yes," he said, "I am doing pretty good these days. I broke my own record selling *The Saturday Evening Post* this week."

"How much is that?" I said.

"I sold 167 copies this week," he said. "Most boys feel lucky if they sell 75 or 100 copies. But not for me."

"How many are there in your family, Johnny?" I said.

"Six counting myself," he said. "There is my father, three smaller brothers and two small sisters."

"Where's your mother?" I said.

"Mother died a year ago," Johnny said.

He stayed in the basement a good one hour sorting out the magazines he wished. I stood by and talked to him as he lifted each copy and inspected it thoroughly. When I asked him if he had made a good sale with the old magazines recently, he said yes. He sold the *Scribner's* Fiftieth Anniversary Issue for sixty cents. Then he said he made several good sales with *Esquire* and a *Vanity Fair* this week.

"You have a smart head, Johnny," I said. "You have found a new way to make money."

Johnny smiled and said nothing. Then he gathered up the fourteen copies he picked out and said he must be going now.

"Johnny," I said, "hereafter you pay two cents a copy. That will be enough."

Johnny looked at me.

"No," he said. "Three cents is all right. You must make a profit, too."

An eleven-year-old boy—I watched him go out with his short business-like stride.

Next day he was back early in the morning. "Back so soon?" I said.

"Yesterday's were all orders," he said. "I want some more today."

"You certainly have a good trade," I said.

"The people know me pretty good. And I know them pretty good," he said. And about ten minutes later he picked out seven copies and said that was all he was taking today.

"I am taking Dad shopping," he said. "I am going to buy a new hat and shoes for him today."

"He must be tickled," I said.

"You bet he is," Johnny said. "He told me to be sure and come home early."

So he said he was taking these seven copies to the customers who ordered them and then run home to get Dad.

Two days later Johnny wanted some more magazines. He said a Mr. Whitman who lived up a block wanted all the magazines with Theodore Dreiser's stories inside. Then he went on talking about other customers of his. Miss White, the school teacher, read Hemingway and he said she would buy back copies with Hemingway stories anytime he brought them in. Some liked Sinclair Lewis, others Saroyan, Faulkner, Steinbeck, Mann, Faith Baldwin, Fannie Hurst, Thomas Wolfe. So it went. It was amazing how an eleven-year-old boy could remember the customer's preferences and not get mixed up.

One day I asked him what he wanted to do when he grew up. He said he wanted a book shop all his own. He said he would handle old books and old magazines as well as the new ones and own the biggest bookstore around the Bay Region.

"That is a good ambition," I said. "You can do it. Just keep up the good work and hold your customers."

On the same day, in the afternoon, he came around to the house holding several packages.

"This is for you," he said, handing over a package. "What is this?" I said.

Johnny laughed. "Open up and see for yourself," he said.

I opened it. It was a book rest, a simple affair but handy.

"I am giving these to all my customers," Johnny said.

"This is too expensive to give away, Johnny," I said. "You will lose all your profits."

"I picked them up cheap," he said. "I'm giving these away so the customers will remember me."

"That is right, too," I said. "You have good sense."

After that he came in about half a dozen times, each time taking with him ten or twelve copies of various magazines. He said he was doing swell. Also, he said he was now selling *Liberty* along with the *Saturday Evening Posts.*

Then for two straight weeks I did not see him once. I could not understand this. He had never missed coming to the house in two or three days. Something must be wrong, I thought. He must be sick, I thought.

One day I saw Johnny at the door. "Hello, Johnny," I said. "Where were you? Were you sick?"

"No. I wasn't sick," Johnny said.

"What's the matter? What happened?" I said.

"I'm moving away," Johnny said. "My father is moving to Los Angeles."

"Sit down, Johnny," I said. "Tell me all about it."

He sat down. He told me what had happened in two weeks. He said his dad went and got married to a woman he, Johnny, did not know. And now, his dad and this woman say they are moving to Los Angeles. And about all there was for him to do was to go along with them.

"I don't know what to say, Johnny," I said.

Johnny said nothing. We sat quietly and watched the time move.

"Too bad you will lose your good trade," I finally said.

"Yes. I know," he said. "But I can sell magazines in Los Angeles."

"Yes, that is true," I said.

Then he said he must be going. I wished him good luck. We shook hands. "I will come and see you again," he said.

"And when I visit Los Angeles some day," I said, "I will see you in the largest bookstore in the city."

Johnny smiled. As he walked away, up the street and out of sight, I saw the last of him walking like a good businessman, walking briskly, energetically, purposefully.

The Brothers

THIS IS REALLY ABOUT GEORGE AND TSUNEO, TWO TINY Japanese boys who are brothers, but I must first mention something about their father for it was through him I came to know something about these two tiny lives. The father is a splendid dentist who has built up a reputation in the city and is doing nicely even in recession. For over a year I have been going to his office every Tuesday morning at ten to do something about my three abscessed teeth. And strangely I came to look forward to these appointments after a while. This is where the two tiny boys, George and Tsuneo, come in.

Tsuneo is three and George is five and they are typical of their age regardless of their nationality. Likely as not they could have been the sons of a German or British or French or Russian or Chinese or American or Eskimo. Their age is of time when their activities are completely of their own sphere and when the adult influence has little to do with their actions unless the child is willing to accede to the adult. I had been going steadily to the office for over two months before the dentist mentioned his sons at home. Before that, the dentist and I liked to talk on every kind of subject. But once the adventure of the two tiny boys was mentioned by the father, little else was of interest. It began so innocently and naturally, the drama of these two tiny lives, and it was not so easily picked up but came slowly to me toward the end or the climax of recent episodes.

Perhaps the source of their struggle between themselves began with George's possession of an old office desk which the father had given to him. That was when the smaller Tsuneo was two years old or not quite two. When Tsuneo reached three there was no old office desk to give him so the father did nothing about it. The father knew the younger son coveted George's desk and was always seen hovering near by as George put away his toys and things in the many drawers of the desk. So the father one day went into a toy shop and brought home a toy desk for Tsuneo. This seemed to appease the younger one and everything was smoothed out, the father thought.

Then one afternoon while he was at the office the mother saw Tsuneo throw the toy desk into a corner. That was the end of the toy desk and the beginning of the struggle of two tiny lives for the coveted office desk, although George was still unaware of it.

While he sat in the living room reading the evening papers every now and then the father looked into the playroom adjoining the living room. He was aware that something was up in the room, although the room was quiet and Tsuneo had not come to him asking for the old office desk. For several nights at a stretch there was little change in the playroom. Then while Father was at the office there was a wild squabble in the playroom. There were no punches struck nor scratches made; the mother had come on the scene in time. The problem was left as it was till Father reached home in the evening.

While the dentist worked on my teeth he told me how he worked out the situation. He said there are four drawers in the desk, three on the side and one just above the knees. He said he made George relinquish the lower drawer to Tsuneo so the younger one, too, would have a part of the desk. Territory, he called it. At that time the Manchurian affair hogged the headlines and everywhere he went there was the talk of war and war clouds. So when we discussed the problem of George and Tsuneo and their struggle it was a timely one. The father had been aware of its relation long before this; that was why he spoke of his two tiny sons and shook his head and smiled. "What barbarians," he would say.

"You have a bigger war right in your home than anywhere else," I said to him one morning from his fine dentist chair.

"Yes, very true," he said.

The dentist was really concerned. He had a time of it as a father. He could not understand how such fierce animals could be his children, to act and react with base motives.

When he said that, I looked at the father. He was a small, delicate man with sensitive hands that are white and tapering and delicate with a lifetime of minute dentistry problems. It really was phenomenal that such a man, an intellect, could be the father of two tiny sons so close to nature. It was something to wonder at. Still, so it was.

Instead of talking about the weather it became a

habit with us, the dentist and I, to greet each other every Tuesday morning with something about George and Tsuneo and their progress into each other's territory. With a twinkle in his eyes, the dentist began calling them the haves and have nots and later, when I became deadly serious about these two tiny ones, I believed the father did not do so bad. Every Tuesday morning there was something new for me to hear. Every Tuesday I was there with interest and alarm.

"Well, how are the boys this week?" I said.

"Tsuneo has taken another drawer of the old desk," said the dentist. "Several nights ago I noticed he has possession of two drawers."

"That leaves two drawers for George," I said.

"Yes," said the dentist, "but this is not the end. The younger one is still eyeing the top drawers which are bigger and roomier."

"Why doesn't George do something about it? Does he stand by and allow Tsuneo to take possession of his drawers?" I said.

"That is where the phenomenon of nature takes hold of each one. Tsuneo, the three-year-old, is the strongest because he has less fear of losing his possession. He is strong and powerful by simply having little and he covets all and stakes all for a gain," the dentist said.

"And George?" I said.

"He is five and lot stronger," the dentist said. "But he has many more things to mind. He must police all his belongings and that takes much of his strength out of him. At five he knows enough to give in a little and lose few than to lose much more by antagonizing."

I laughed. "At five and three there is a greater war going on than all the adult wars recorded in history."

"Yes," said the dentist, "wars of inherent nature remain unrecorded and are vaster in number."

From the day Tsuneo grabbed hold of the first drawer there was no beginning to speak of and definitely no end to the whole matter although one episode such as this may end and be forgotten. Also, there is no end nor beginning in possession of things. According to their father, George and Tsuneo had in their possession all the things they were to require and receive later. When the struggle for the drawers of the desk commenced, simultaneously everything in their range and knowledge began to move. George had a half dozen toy autos; so did Tsuneo. That much was equal in possession. After that it was all George's. He had three toy trains while Tsuneo had one. George had four color books and five boxes of crayons, and three brand new pencils. Tsuneo had one color book and two boxes of crayons, one new pencil and an old short piece. So it went with marbles, zee nuts, wood blocks, cap pistols, and all the rest of the playthings they possessed.

One Tuesday morning the dentist said Tsuneo had one more drawer of his own, his third one. This time he said George got real mad and if he had not been home early there would have been a real fight. He said he subsided both parties promising tricycles for Christmas.

"You have a job keeping both sides contented," I said.

"The trouble with it all is George is always ahead. He is two years ahead and will keep it that way as long as he can," he said.

Several weeks later the inevitable fight occurred. It upset the father so much all he did to my teeth that morning was to brush my teeth with some sticky paste to take the film off. All the while he kept clucking his tongue as if the world had turned upside down.

"When did it happen?" I said.

"Last night," he said. "I made them go to bed without supper. That was their punishment."

The fight was over the last drawer George had in possession in the old desk. One of Tsuneo's eyes was blackened and George bore marks of scratches and bruises from numerous kicks. The fight was short and brief as Mother came running on the scene. They kicked and screamed and scratched and the house was a bedlam.

When the father came home in the night the boys were for peace, at least temporarily. Tsuneo, the little one, was still defiant a little but George was all for settling peacefully.

So this morning, the father said, the boys sat down at the table and ate an extra bowl full of corn flakes. They sat quietly and ate their breakfast and for a while the father thought there had been no such thing as fight between them.

But as the boys sat in front of him the father did not like the quietness found in time and place and as he watched his tiny sons quietly gobbling up the corn flakes, he knew that behind silence, behind little heads, their little eyes are for coveted things and their hands are to paw and smash, and the brewing trouble which is the worry and the sadness of the earth is once again stirring.

Tomorrow and Today

HATSUYE IS THE ELDER SISTER OF MINEKO, THE PRET-
ty one. They live in the house above the Yokohama
Fish Company on Eighth Street. While Mineko works
uptown in an art goods store, Hatsuye remains home
and relieves mother of housekeeping and cooking and
sewing. She has been doing the same routine for eight
years or so but she never squawks.

There is little that I can do to romanticize Hatsuye
and show her off like I might do for her younger sister
who is little and pretty and alert. All that one can say
about Hatsuye is that she is plain and is a swell home-
maker. To be crude about the whole thing you would
say she is ugly, the ugliest young girl you ever saw.

About once a week there is a heartening lift in the
life of Hatsuye. For example, she went this week to
see Clark Gable in *Test Pilot* at the Fox-Oakland. I
don't believe she has missed a picture of Clark Gable's
since she began to notice him. In her room she has
copies of old *Photoplay, Hollywood,* and *Screenland,*
containing pictures of Clark Gable. She is too timid
to clip out his face and tack it on the wall as Mineko
does her favorite, Robert Taylor. So Hatsuye does the
next best thing. She collects the old copies and sets
them aside in a special rack. When she is feeling pretty
low or feels like singing and dancing inside of her, she
goes to the special rack and pulls out the magazines
and studies the photographs.

In her quiet way Hatsuye envies her pretty sister who is always coming in and going out of the house, flitting here and there without a moment's rest. I believe she would go overboard if she could do such a thing and adopt Mineko's attitude toward life, toward men, and everything else; facing things directly and directly treating them. She is sure Mineko must be happier by being concerned solely for the present and the rest may go to the blazes. Her younger sister's attitude spells carefree and buoyance. Of course Mineko has everything coming her way; good clothes, many men to take her out, good figure, good sport, and very little worry over anything going on about her.

It is absurd to think that she, Hatsuye, could ever stand in a similar position and become another Mineko. To her, the present, that of facing matters directly, rarely does good for her. All that she can do with what she has is to look into the future that is dim, unknown, and at least hopeful. That is what she does when there is a heartening lift inside of her to see Clark Gable doing his stuff on the screen.

The quarrel between Hatsuye and Mineko came over some petty incident that would be ignored another time. Perhaps it was over the mess that is always Mineko's room or what a rotten piece of ironing Hatsuye had done on Mineko's dress. One way or the other does not matter. About the only thing that does matter about the quarrel is the way Mineko said the pretty obvious thing about Hatsuye, which came from hate and fact.

She said at the heat of the quarrel, "You are ugly, Hatsuye! You're so ugly no man will look at you."

With that crack from Mineko all else stopped. Hatsuye, who was defiant till then, stopped, becoming at once colorless, weak, and dull. She had known right along she was no beauty. She acknowledged herself being not even fairly pretty. So when her sister abruptly said she was ugly she did not dread it. She had expected a retort of that sort. But an acknowledgment that she was ugly through and through and was hopeless made her ill. She did not dread being ugly herself; that she accepted. But for others to see in her all ugliness gave her no lead and all hopelessness ahead.

For weeks after that, when she regularly attended the movies and watched Clark Gable and others, the old romantic air was gone, and the romantic hope that she had so cherished looked like a joke. For a while, everything looked like a satire and a stab into a person like herself. Everything was ridiculous and miserable. She had nothing to gain and hope for. She did not even enjoy seeing Clark Gable cavorting before her in romantic roles. Up in her room she sat and looked over the photos of Clark Gable and shook her head, waiting for the future to descend.

Later, when Hatsuye had somewhat recovered and Mineko had lost her enmity and Clark Gable had regained his popularity in her eyes, she began to move around the house like her old self. She began to sneak out once or twice a week to the theater and though she could not be so hopeful and intimate as before, she found that she still possessed a dim hope that something might happen some day. Naturally, she does not expect to meet or speak to Clark Gable, she would not hope or even want that. But if sometime in Hollywood she would see him arriving at a first movie showing, alighting from his classy automobile, that would be very nice.

The interesting part of Hatsuye is that she is hopeful in spite of the fact that she is hopeless. She knows she is no beauty but she is hopeful that she is not all ugliness to others. That is something. And when she has but a dim hope of future or of Clark Gable, she is still in possession of something alive to work with and that is something.

Today is Hatsuye's washday. From my back porch I can see her moving about in her yard. In about twenty minutes she must return to the kitchen and prepare the supper for the family. In the morning she had finished her weekly housekeeping. Tomorrow she has sewing to do and ironing and washing in the afternoon. On Saturday night when she is through with the duties she will go to a movie where a favorite like Clark Gable may be playing. When she returns from the theater she will take a hot bath and retire.

When one has been around the neighborhood a while, the routine is familiar and is not emphasized. It appears dull and colorless. But in this routine there is the breath-taking suspense that is alive and enormous, although the outcome and prospect of it is a pretty obvious thing. Although her hope may be unfilled there is no reason why she cannot be a lover of Clark Gable.

Hatsuye is back in the kitchen watching over a steaming pan of rice, cutting *sukiyaki* meat for a *sukiyaki,* and washing the leek and cutting them in small pieces. This sort of stuff is going on every minute, every hour, every day in the house and Hatsuye is still going strong. While she is moving about day in and day out it is not whether she is brave and courageous or tragic and pathetic that is important about her life, but it is her day that is present and the day that is tomorrow which is her day and which will not be.